Also in the

series:

Canyon Chaos

Rainforest Rampage

Desert Disaster

First published in 2013 by Curious Fox,
an imprint of Capstone Global Library Limited,
7 Pilgrim Street, London, EC4V 6LB
Registered company number: 6695582

www.curious-fox.com

Series created by Hothouse Fiction
www.hothousefiction.com

The author's moral rights are hereby asserted.

Cover illustration by Spooky Pooka
Cover design by Mandy Norman

ISBN 978 1 78202 050 9

1 3 5 7 9 10 8 6 4 2

A CIP catalogue for this book is available from the British Library.

Typeset in Avenir by Hothouse Fiction Ltd

Printed and bound in the United Kingdom by CPI Group (UK) Ltd,
Croydon, CR0 4YY

MIX
Paper from
responsible sources
FSC® C020471

With special thanks to David Grant

CHAPTER ONE
Destination Unknown

The vast steel door of the airship clanged shut and the airlock sealed it with a hiss and a metallic thud. The robot racers were on their way.

Jimmy Roberts hurried to one of the tiny circular portholes. He headed past the workstations where each of the racers' teams were working feverishly on their state-of-the-art robots. Jimmy's own robot, Cabbie, was already updated and his grandpa, Wilfred Roberts, was sat next to him with a celebratory cup of tea.

By the time Jimmy got to the little round window, they were way above the ground.

He peered down from the airship at his little house. He could just about make out the garden shed where Grandpa had built Cabbie out of a rusty old taxi cab and bits of scrap material.

It had been nearly two months since Lord Leadpipe had announced that he would be opening up his world-famous racing championship to children for the first time. In a whirlwind few days, Jimmy had learned that his jolly old grandpa was actually a genius robot inventor who used to work for the most secret department of the Secret Services. Grandpa had built Cabbie for Jimmy so that he could compete in the Robot Races against some of the best robots in the world.

And now, here they were, on their way to the third stage of the competition.

Jimmy could hardly believe he was a robot racer, no matter how many times he thought about it. Even when he said it out loud.

The house and garden shed got smaller and smaller as the airship climbed, until Jimmy's hometown of Smedingham was so far away that it looked like a toy town. The cars driving along the busy streets seemed to crawl over them like tiny bugs. And then they were high in the clouds and Jimmy could see nothing at all.

"Hey, Jimmy!"

Jimmy turned to see Sammy walking towards him. Sammy – Samir Bahur from Egypt – was one of the other competitors.

Jimmy grinned and gave his friend a high five. "Hey, Sammy, how's it going?"

"Good, thank you," said Sammy in his strong North African accent. "And how are you? Have you recovered from our adventure in the jungle?"

"I think so," said Jimmy with a smile. "And I'm ready for another one."

"In the jungle?" asked Sammy.

"Wherever we're going," said Jimmy.

Jimmy, Sammy and the other robot racers had competed in the dark depths of the South American jungle in their last race – on a track that had introduced them to scary creatures, lakes of quicksand and even an ancient underground temple.

Jimmy noticed Sammy looking over his shoulder at Cabbie, his eyebrows lifting in surprise. Jimmy reckoned his friend was checking Cabbie out, looking for modifications or new gadgets. While Sammy was busy looking at Cabbie, Jimmy snatched a glance over *Sammy's* shoulder to see what changes had been made to his robot, Maximus, since the jungle race. The vast hoverbot looked just the same – although it was a lot cleaner now that the jungle mud and swamp splats had been hosed off. Maybe the enormous propellers that powered the hoverbot were slightly larger than before… And was that a new hatch on the front, concealing some amazing new gadget?

"You have been practising your driving?" asked Sammy.

"Well…" said Jimmy. He didn't want to say that he had driven Cabbie just once since he and Sammy had roared to a shared victory in the Rainforest Rampage leg of the championship. But there just weren't that many places in his home town of Smedingham where a kid could take a rocket-powered robot for a spin.

Jimmy's one test drive around the back streets of his estate had ended with a neighbour's garden fence on fire and some nasty burn marks on their patio umbrella, thanks to his upgraded rocket-boosters. Jimmy grimaced at the thought. Luckily the Fire

Brigade had arrived quickly – and while they were there, they'd rescued the neighbour's terrified cat, which had run up a tree and was refusing to come down. Grandpa and Jimmy had agreed he should lay off the driving practice for a while.

As Jimmy and Sammy talked, all the other competitors came wandering over. There was Princess Kako from Japan in her signature silver leathers, her hair scraped back and tied in a neat bun, straight-faced and silent as usual. Beside her, Chip, an African-American boy, strode along in his usual T-shirt, jeans and baseball cap. He was chatting to Missy, the loud Australian, who was shouting back at him at her usual deafening volume. Her wild, red curly hair hung loose around her shoulders and Jimmy could see the usual grease smears on her denim dungarees and face, showing the hard work she'd been doing to improve her robot racer, Monster.

"Hey, Jimmy!" she bellowed. "How's it going?" She thumped Jimmy on the back so hard he stopped breathing for a few seconds.

"Fine," wheezed Jimmy. "Thanks for asking. How are you?"

"Couldn't be better, mate!" yelled Missy, thumping him again.

Jimmy tried to speak but ended up just nodding.

"Good to see you all again," beamed Chip, looking around the group of drivers. "Hey! Where'd Horace go?"

A sudden blast from Cabbie's horn made them all turn sharply. They spun round to see Horace jumping away from Cabbie. He had blond hair and tanned skin from all the holidays he went on with his wealthy parents, and perfectly straight, white teeth which he used to pull a smug grin whenever he had the chance.

Jimmy and Horace had gone to school together back in Smedingham, but they'd never been friends.

"Ha," Horace laughed nervously, trying to pretend he hadn't been spying on someone else's robot. "What a *charming* horn that is." He strolled back to where the other drivers stood. "Hello again, Jimmy." He grinned, his white teeth gleaming. "Scabbie's looking like he's ready for the scrapyard, as usual."

"Had a good look, did you, Horace?" asked Jimmy.

"There wasn't much to see," sneered Horace.

"So where do you think we will be racing this

time?" asked Sammy, interrupting them before they could argue any further.

"No idea," said Jimmy, turning his attention back to the others.

"I am hoping for some sand," smiled Sammy. "A nice desert, perhaps."

"Or a beach in the Caribbean!" suggested Chip. "Miles of white sand, clear blue sea..."

"I'd like a big city," said Princess Kako. "Smooth, wide, floodlit city streets are much better than the dark and mud of the jungle. And also the shops and restaurants and hotels..." she added with a faraway look in her eyes.

"Don't be soft!" bellowed Missy, rubbing her hands together excitedly. "I want somewhere a bit more exciting than that. Up a volcano or down a mineshaft or—"

"Yes!" said Jimmy, his brain fizzing with excitement. "Or through some underground caves. Or over the Himalayas!"

"What about you, Horace?" asked Chip. "What do you want?"

"Zoom can cope with any terrain," sneered Horace.

"And my NASA engineers are prepared for anything. So, unlike you losers, I don't really care."

"As long as there isn't any quicksand, eh, Horace?" giggled Missy.

The others burst out laughing, remembering how Horace had found himself in a sticky situation during their last race.

Horace didn't join in with the laughter. He narrowed his eyes and gritted his shiny teeth. Jimmy couldn't help but think that the Australian girl would pay for that comment. Horace was definitely one competitor who knew how to hold a grudge.

"Hey, Jimmy," said Sammy, "maybe we will have another adventure together like last time." He laughed. "But I am hoping not. I think this race would be better if we don't see so many snakes, no?"

"I thought we were going to spend the rest of our lives stuck in that ruined temple," replied Jimmy with a grin.

"And the rest of our lives would not have been a long time," said Sammy. "When you are in a booby-trapped temple and the walls are trying to squash you, it is not so good for your health."

"All right, all right, you two," shrieked Missy, cutting Sammy off with a playful nudge in the ribs. "We had to listen to this all the way back from the jungle. Don't make us hear it all over again! We know you're Sammy's biggest fan, Jimmy, and Sammy thinks you're the koala's pyjamas. But remember, we're all competing against each other here, eh?"

"Don't worry," said Jimmy, rubbing his ribs where Missy had poked him. "You'll all be eating my dust on the next race."

"I think not, slow bus." replied Sammy. "*I* will be winning the next stage."

At that, the others burst out laughing.

"I think you mean 'slow coach'," Jimmy told him.

"Oops," Sammy said. "My English is still a little rusty, I think."

As the rest of the group continued to chatter amongst themselves, Jimmy began to feel a thrill shooting up his spine at the thought of the next race. But then he remembered what Grandpa had said as they had waited for Lord Leadpipe's airship to come and collect them.

"You're in first place on the leaderboard, but there

are four more races to be run," he had said, his white moustache bouncing up and down over his top lip. "And goodness only knows what ridiculous nonsense that old fool, Lord *Loonpipe*, has got rattling around in his tiny brain. He could have planned anything for this next race, so keep your wits about you and one eye on your rear-view mirror." And then he had given Jimmy a big hug.

The smile slowly faded from Jimmy's lips, and instead he felt a jolt of fear squirming in his belly. Now, as he looked around at the other competitors, he started to worry. *What if I'm not prepared? What if Cabbie can't handle the conditions? Lord Leadpipe could have planned anything...*

A cold sweat spread up Jimmy's back and suddenly his stomach climbed into his throat.

Then his ears started popping.

Jimmy realized that it wasn't fear sending his stomach somersaulting around his body. It was the airship descending.

"We're landing!" shouted Chip.

They each rushed over to one of the little round portholes around the edge of the airship's enormous hangar and peered out.

"I can't see a thing," shrieked Missy.

"Me neither," said Sammy.

Jimmy stared out into the whiteness of solid cloud as the airship shuddered, and there was a *thud* beneath Jimmy's feet which made him jump.

"I think we've landed," said Chip.

"Nah," said Missy. "I can still see clouds. We're still in the air, for sure."

Jimmy pressed his face up against the window and tried to peer out, but his breath kept misting up the glass. All he could see was blank, white space.

"Maybe we've landed on top of a mountain," cried Chip. "A mountain so high that we're racing up in the clouds!"

"Perhaps Lord Leadpipe's built a track in the sky!" cried Sammy.

"You idiots!" sneered Horace.

"So where are we then, Mr Clever Pants?" snapped Missy.

Horace was just about to reply when he was interrupted by a creaking sound, a loud metallic groan.

The vast steel door of the airship juddered.

All six competitors stood and stared open-mouthed as the crack of daylight at the top of the door began to grow.

"I think we're about to find out," said Jimmy.

CHAPTER TWO
A Couple of Surprises

Jimmy stared wide-eyed as the huge steel door of the airship was lowered on its huge steel hinges. He narrowed his eyes as the crack of white light got wider and brighter. Then a blast of freezing air hit him in the face and a flurry of white specks flew in, coating his eyebrows and hair in a fine white frost. Jimmy flinched, wiping the flakes out of his eyes. He peered again through the huge airship doorway into the whiteness.

It's not clouds, he thought to himself. *It's snow! Miles and miles of snow.*

As his eyes became more accustomed to the

dazzling glare coming from beyond the hangar doors he could see the white surface more clearly as it stretched off to the horizon in every direction.

Even the clanging and banging and shouting of the team mechanics stopped as they all put down their tools and came to stare out at the scene.

Another sudden sharp gust of freezing air whipped through the doorway, sending a pile of paper blueprints flying through the air and flinging a stack of empty oil cans to the ground. Behind him, Jimmy could hear angry voices cursing, and several mechanics came scurrying past to clean up the mess. The poster that Jimmy's team sponsor, *That's Shallot!*, had pinned to his workstation wall was ripped loose. It fluttered around amongst the tools for a second, before another gust whisked it outside through the doorway.

Jimmy gasped at the cold as the howling wind hurled snow in every direction. His teeth began to chatter and he wished he was wearing a coat.

"Look!" said Chip.

As the wind dropped, the snow thinned slightly and Jimmy could just make out the shape of a white dome against the grey sky.

"It's an igloo!" shrieked Missy. "A huge igloo!"

"And look…" Sammy gasped.

A figure was emerging from the little tunnel at the front of the igloo, slowly squeezing its way out into the frozen landscape. The person stopped for a moment and looked around, then headed straight for the airship, stamping along in heavy brown boots and a huge furry hooded coat.

"Anyone speak Eskimo?" said Missy anxiously.

"I think it's called Inuit," said Chip. "And, no. Not a word. Whaddya think he wants?"

"Maybe he wants to know why someone's parked an enormous airship next to his house," said Princess Kako.

"I think he's angry," whimpered Horace, crouching down behind Jimmy, his teeth chattering. "He's getting closer!"

Horace was right. The figure was coming straight for them.

It even raised a hand and waved at them.

Then it slowly pulled back its hood … to reveal a man wearing a monocle, which glinted in the light from the blinding white snow. It was Lord Ludwick Leadpipe!

"Greetings, competitors!" he shouted over the noise of the gale. "Welcome to the Arctic Circle. If you would like to get in your racers and join me out on the snow, I'll tell you all about the next leg of the competition."

It took a moment for it to sink in. The competitors turned to each other, grinning in amazement, before hurrying off to their robots.

"We're in the Arctic!" said Jimmy as he hopped into Cabbie's cockpit.

"I-I-I-I-know!" stammered Cabbie, his pistons spluttering in the sub-zero temperature.

"You'll soon warm up," said Jimmy, wondering if his teeth were chattering from the cold or from excitement.

The pit area echoed with the sound of engines roaring as the racers fired up their robots and prepared to head out onto the ice.

Jimmy and Cabbie were out first. They eased out of their workstation and made their way towards the doorway. It was already gathering a thick layer of snow. Slowly they edged onto the steep ramp and Cabbie immediately began to slide. Jimmy stamped on the brakes, but it didn't stop them hurtling down the slope.

"Whoaaaa," shuddered Cabbie, skidding out across the ice and spinning to a stop.

"Erm, I think we're going to need some different tyres," said Jimmy, trying to keep calm.

He watched the other racers follow them down the ramp from the airship. Missy and Monster shot out onto the slippery ground, Monster's huge tyres spinning and spraying snow everywhere while Missy howled with laughter. Next came Chip and Dug, moving surely and slowly, his caterpillar tracks gripping the ice with ease.

Sammy and his hoverbot, Maximus, sat nervously at the top of the ramp for a moment before gliding smoothly over the ice and coming to a controlled stop next to Cabbie and Jimmy.

Princess Kako and her robobike Lightning followed very slowly and carefully, Kako adding extra stability by stabbing the sharp points of her heavy biker boots into the ice.

Lastly Horace and Zoom rocketed down the ramp and across the ice, screeching to a dramatic stop as Horace pulled a handbrake turn.

"This ice is no problem for the SuperGrip tyres my NASA team have developed!" he shouted out his window.

Soon all the parents and mechanics joined the racers, wrapped up in padded coats and boots and scarves and gloves and fur hats. Herding them like a sheep dog was Joshua Johnson, the Robot Co-ordinator, dressed like a yeti in a brown furry jacket, brown furry trousers and brown furry boots. Joshua's huge smile looked even bigger than usual, and Jimmy couldn't help wondering if it had been frozen in position.

Jimmy waved at Grandpa. At least, he thought it was Grandpa – it looked like his moustache poking out of the fur-lined hood.

Grandpa came over and Jimmy opened Cabbie's window.

"You look cosy, Grandpa," he smiled.

"Typical Loonpipe!" mumbled Grandpa through his furry hood. "He has to put on a show. Why can't he just hold the race on a normal racetrack?"

"Drivers," announced Joshua Johnson through a megaphone. "Please exit your vehicles for your race briefing."

Jimmy got out of Cabbie and shivered. Grandpa handed him a thick, furry coat and Jimmy wrapped himself up in it quickly.

"Attention, please!" called Lord Leadpipe's voice.

Jimmy and Grandpa looked around to see where the voice was coming from.

"Look!" said Jimmy. He pointed to where Lord Leadpipe was standing on a vast block of ice with a microphone in his hand, surrounded by camerabots who had appeared from another section of the huge airship.

"Here we go again," mumbled Grandpa.

"Racers," continued Lord Leadpipe. "Welcome to the Arctic stage of the Robot Races Championship! There are three – yes, *three*! – different tracks which you can choose to follow in this race."

The competitors all shifted nervously from foot to foot at this unexpected surprise.

"There will be no pit stops on any of the three

tracks, so you should choose carefully," warned Lord Leadpipe, wagging a warning finger of his fur glove at the competitors. "And play to your strengths. The first route you can choose," he continued, a grin stealing across his face, "will take you over the Arctic Ocean, navigating your way through the narrow channels between the towering ice cliffs. Fall in and you face the dark, ice-cold depths of the sea."

Jimmy swallowed hard and tried not to shiver.

"The second route," said Lord Leadpipe, "is on land over the snows of Greenland. Should you choose this route, you will need to be constantly vigilant for snow covered crevasses – huge cracks in the earth's surface, sometimes up to half a mile deep. Not to mention the howling, freezing winds stirring up snowstorms which can cause you to lose your way in the blink of an eye."

"None of them sound too appealing so far," whispered Grandpa.

"And the third route," continued Lord Leadpipe, "will take you across the frozen sheets of ice covering the sea. The ice could give way at any moment," he added with a grim smile. "And, of course," he added, "I hardly need to mention that on all three routes there is the possibility of hypothermia, snow blindness and frostbite – after all, it is a bit nippy out here, isn't it?"

"Sounds like it's going to be a barrel of laughs from start to finish," Cabbie joked next to Jimmy.

Lightning, meanwhile, was showing off. In a blur of flying snow and flashing black metal, his wheels folded in and he transformed into a sled – complete with snowplough at the front and a huge single rocket-thruster at the rear – and then back to robobike again.

Monster retaliated by lifting her front grille and pushing out a vast snowplough that looked like it could clear an iceberg. At the controls, Missy grinned proudly.

Chip's robot racer, Dug, raised his crane arm and swung it in a circle over their heads before bringing it down with an almighty crash on the ice, sending a metre-wide crack ripping through the ice as far as the eye could see.

"We've got some work to do if we're going to win this one, Cabbie!" said Jimmy, giving his robot an affectionate pat on the bonnet.

"I'm reconfiguring my software already," said

Cabbie, his processors whirring away somewhere behind his dashboard.

"You have just one day to prepare for the race," said Lord Leadpipe. "But in the meantime, I have a couple of surprises for you," he said. "The first is this. The winner of tomorrow's race will not only receive ten points to add to their score on the leaderboard, but he or she will also be presented with a very special prize from Leadpipe Industries. A very special prize indeed."

Lord Leadpipe paused to let this news sink in.

"I bet it's some kind of upgrade," said Jimmy, his eyes glistening with excitement. "A top-of-the-range robo-upgrade—"

"—which will be mine when I beat you losers by miles," said Horace, appearing suddenly at Jimmy's shoulder.

"We'll see about that," muttered Jimmy, grinding his teeth.

"Not that I need any upgrades, of course." Horace continued, more smugly than ever. "Zoom is already fully top-of-the-range from top to bottom."

"And the other surprise..." said Lord Leadpipe,

pausing until everyone had held their breath, "will be revealed a little later on."

And with a final wink to the contestants he leaped down from his ice block and strolled back to the igloo.

"That man is one washer short of an engine cylinder," Grandpa muttered.

Jimmy grinned. "Who cares! It's nearly time for the next race!"

CHAPTER THREE
Three's a Team

Jimmy ran to get into Cabbie. Grandpa followed and got in alongside as Jimmy fired up the robot's engine.

"Can you believe it, Grandpa?" said Jimmy, puffing with excitement as they cruised back up the ramp and into Cabbie's workstation. "There's a special prize for winning this race. A Leadpipe Industries upgrade, I reckon."

"Yes, yes," said Grandpa, showing no interest at all as Jimmy parked and secured the handbrake. "I don't think we'll be needing any of their rubbish, thank you very much," he continued as they clambered out. "Although I could probably get something useful out of it. Something to make the auto-vacuum get around the carpet a bit quicker, perhaps..."

"Don't worry, Scabbie," came Horace's voice echoing across the airship. "I don't think there are any snakes in the Arctic so you won't need to spend half the race screaming like a baby. You know, like you did in the rainforest." Horace's head popped up from behind Zoom, and he threw his head back and laughed. The noise was like the hee-haw of a particularly annoying donkey.

"You'll be the one screaming like a baby when we win, Horace!" Jimmy shouted back.

"You tell him, Jimmy," said Cabbie. "We'll show him what Jimmy Roberts and Cabbie are made of!"

"Yeah?" Horace called back.

"Yeah!" shouted Cabbie, shaking so much that Jimmy thought he might blow a gasket. "Who's first on the championship leaderboard? Me and Jimmy! Where did you and Zoom come in the Rainforest Rampage, eh?"

Horace opened and closed his mouth like a fish out of water, but he couldn't think of a good response. Instead, he stamped his foot with a *thud* and disappeared into the crowd of NASA engineers surrounding Zoom.

Jimmy bit his lip and clenched his fists. He hated arguing. But he couldn't help Horace getting under his skin. Just the thought of watching his smarmy face at the top of the podium made Jimmy feel a surge of competitiveness.

"There's no way we're going to let them beat us," he muttered to himself.

"It's not all about winning, you know, my boy," whispered Grandpa, resting a comforting hand on Jimmy's shoulder. "You just do your best and I'll be proud of you."

"What's all this shouting?" came Lord Leadpipe's voice. He was marching up the ramp into the airship, still in his fur hood and boots. "Bit of friendly banter; a dash of the competitive spirit! That's the ticket, racers, good to see a bit of passion and fire in your bellies. That's what this competition needs."

"Now hold on a minute, Leadpipe," said Grandpa, stepping in front of Jimmy as though to protect him. "I don't need you encouraging my grandson to act like that! What kind of a role model d'you think you are?"

Lord Leadpipe frowned, like he was struggling to work out a complex calculation in his head. "I say, Wilfred, I don't know quite what you're talking about—"

"Never mind pretending you're all innocent," Grandpa continued, ignoring the billionaire's protests. "You wander around in that ridiculous furry outfit, looking like a stuffed grizzly bear, drag us to the ends of the earth with no warning at all – I haven't even brought a pair of woolly winter socks. What do you think this cold is going to do to my chilblains?"

"I—" Lord Leadpipe tried to say, but there was no stopping Grandpa.

"D'you know what the temperature is out there? It's minus twenty! I think you could have warned us that you were—"

"I—" tried Lord Leadpipe again.

"Grandpa!" Jimmy tried to interrupt.

"—landing us in the middle of a blizzard," continued Grandpa. "It's completely irresponsible to bring children to a dangerous place like this and expect them to—"

"Grandpa!" bellowed Jimmy.

Finally Grandpa fell silent, his red cheeks puffing plumes of fog into the icy air.

"I think Lord Leadpipe wants to say something," Jimmy said in a quieter voice.

"*Really?*" said Grandpa, as though he had no intention of listening.

"I just wanted to say," said Lord Leadpipe, "that I have made special arrangements to help you deal with the ... er ... chilly circumstances in which you find yourself. My robot co-ordinator, Joshua Johnson, will be coming to see you soon with an array of thermal clothing to keep you warm, including my brand-new invention – a pair of Leadpipe Industries' very own HotFoot™ thermal socks. Oh yes, there he is now." Lord Leadpipe pointed to the far end of the workshop.

Jimmy glanced over at Sammy and Maximus. Joshua Johnson had just arrived at Sammy's pit area. The robot co-ordinator looked even stranger than the last time Jimmy had seen him. From the waist up, he looked like his usual self in a dark blazer with the gold 'L' for Leadpipe on the breast pocket and a bright green cravat round his neck. From the waist down he was still wearing brown furry trousers and furry boots. He looked half-dressed for a part in *Goldilocks and the Three Bears*. With Joshua were three men in brown overalls, unloading towers of cardboard boxes from a huge trolley.

"One box of thermal underwear," Joshua was saying, reading from his clipboard. "Fourteen pairs of HotFoot™ thermal socks ... four pairs of snow boots..."

"And that's not all," Lord Leadpipe continued. "My second surprise of the day is that each racer is being assigned a mechanic."

"A mechanic?" blustered Grandpa, his cheeks reddening again. "We've got one of those, thank you. *Me!*"

"Yes, yes, Wilfred, but this is an *extra* mechanic," explained Lord Leadpipe quietly and patiently, "to help you prepare for the extreme Arctic racing conditions which your grandson will be facing. And not just any mechanic. Even as we speak, six of the finest pit-stop mechanics are leaving Leadpipe Racing HQ in a robocopter."

"Really?" cried Jimmy. "Wow! I wonder which one

we'll be working with, Grandpa." His stomach fizzed with excitement. Some of those mechanics were almost as famous as the drivers they worked for: Ryan the Wrench, Easy-Grease McGraw, Pete Webber – they could change a tyre in under three seconds with one hand while refuelling a pair of turbo rocket-boosters with the other. Rain or shine, hurricane or heat wave, those mechanics were amazing!

"I don't want anyone else meddling with Cabbie," Grandpa grumbled. "I don't want some young whippersnapper poking around under his bonnet with a spanner, breaking things and undoing all my good work."

"But, Grandpa," said Jimmy urgently, "it would be good to have some help. We've only got a day to get ready for the race and the Robot Races' mechanics know all about racing in the Arctic."

Leadpipe nodded. "Yes. We were up here two years ago," he said. "For the final leg of the championship when Big Al and Crusher had that incident with a polar bear."

"Please, Grandpa," pleaded Jimmy. "With a Robot Races' mechanic on the team, we'll be much better prepared for the race!"

There was a long pause. Jimmy held his breath.

"All right, then," Grandpa sighed eventually. "I suppose I could do with a little help. It might be nice to have someone a little younger to carry those heavy snow tyres ... and make the tea. When is he getting here, Leadpipe, this mechanic of yours?"

Leadpipe pulled a gold watch on a chain out from the inside of his fur-lined jacket. "In fifty-eight minutes," he said.

"An hour?" blustered Grandpa. "Tell him to get a move on. We've got a race to get ready for!"

CHAPTER FOUR
Meet Pete

"The question is," said Grandpa, "which route should we take? Over the ice, through the snow or across the sea?"

Jimmy and Grandpa were looking at a map of the three possible race routes on the Cabcom, Cabbie's communication system. Jimmy sat in the driver's seat, both hands gripping the steering wheel, while Grandpa leaned in through the passenger-side window. His eyes were narrowed, deep in thought.

"The ice is fast." Jimmy nodded thoughtfully.

"But slippery," added Grandpa. "One false move and you're skidding into the sea."

"The snow track's much shorter," said Jimmy.

"But it'll be very slow-going with all those snowdrifts," said Grandpa.

"And the crevasses," added Cabbie. "If you fall down one of them, you don't come back up in a hurry." He shuddered so hard at the thought of disappearing down a freezing cold chasm that his windows started to rattle. "What about the sea track?" he asked. "I bet none of the others will pick that! We'd have the place to ourselves. Rolling along through the waves..."

"Have you disconnected your huge computer brain?" said Grandpa in astonishment. "You're only just waterproof!"

"I've got an EFD!" replied Cabbie indignantly.

"The Emergency Flotation Device?" said Jimmy. "The one Grandpa made out of our old rubber dinghy?"

"Yup," said Cabbie.

"Cabbie," said Jimmy with a hint of impatience, "the E stands for *Emergency*. It means it's for emergency use only."

"It'll be fine!" exclaimed Cabbie. "It's tough as old boots, that EFD. Like me. We could do it, Jimmy!"

"No, we couldn't," said Jimmy, with a faint smile at Cabbie's enthusiasm. "Even if it did keep us afloat, we wouldn't get anywhere fast on it. We'd just be drifting around, bobbing up and down when we ought to be racing ahead and winning."

Cabbie went quiet for a moment. "Let's do the snow, let's do the snow!" he said with renewed excitement.

"I don't know, Cabbie. Don't you think we'd be better off on the ice?" said Jimmy.

"I want to do the snow! I want to do the snow!" shouted Cabbie.

"We've got to pick the best route," Jimmy said determindly. "I want Lord Leadpipe's special prize."

Grandpa rolled his eyes. "It's probably an air freshener or a little Leadpipe doll to hang off Cabbie's rear-view mirror."

"No, Grandpa, it's a really *special* prize. Lord Leadpipe said so."

"Loonpipe says a lot of things," said Grandpa grimly, "and most of them are nonsense."

"It's probably a brand-new robot racer," sighed Cabbie. "A top-of-the-range, super-high-tech shiny, spanking new robot racer." Cabbie sighed again. "Don't worry about me, Jimmy, I'll be fine. I can always go back to being a taxi…"

"What are you talking about!?" exclaimed Jimmy. "I don't care if it's a space rocket from the twenty-fifth century! I'm not racing in any robot except you, Cabbie. We're a team and that's that."

"Really?" said Cabbie.

"Really," said Jimmy firmly.

Grandpa put an arm round Jimmy's shoulder and squeezed, a proud smile beaming on his face – and Cabbie seemed to get a few centimetres taller as his tyres inflated with pride.

Behind them someone cleared their throat.

Jimmy and Grandpa jumped and turned round to find someone looking at them. He was a mountain of a man, easily over six feet tall with a bright red baseball cap on backwards. Huge muscles bulged from the short sleeves of his check shirt.

"Jimmy Roberts?" said the man in a quiet growl.

Jimmy's mouth fell open. "You're— you're— you're— you're—" he stammered.

"Who are you?" asked Grandpa politely.

"He's Pete Webber!" cried Jimmy. "He's Big Al and Crusher's pit-stop mechanic! He's the best!"

Pete Webber nodded just once, but said nothing.

"I'm Wilfred Roberts, Jimmy's grandfather and Cabbie's inventor," said Grandpa, smiling and shaking Pete's hand.

"Pleased to meet you," growled Pete Webber in a voice so low it sounded like he was at the bottom of a very deep coal mine.

"Have you— are you— will you...?" said Jimmy.

"You must be the mechanic Lord Leadpipe said would be coming to work with us," said Grandpa.

Pete nodded again, just once as before.

"*Really?*" said Jimmy, his voice so loud and high with excitement it made Cabbie jump.

Pete nodded for a third time. "I've been thinking about these Arctic conditions you'll be racing in," he said. "Now, I've seen Jimmy and Cabbie race—"

"Really?" Jimmy gasped. "You've seen us? Really?" He tried not to explode with happiness.

Pete bobbed his head again before continuing, "So I think I've got some ideas that will help you two."

"Oh, good," Grandpa smiled. "So have I. I've been

thinking about additional antifreeze in the coolant, probably some modifications to the vents to maintain engine temperature, and I've been toying with the idea of a new spoiler to improve traction."

Pete nodded his approval. "Have you thought about reconfiguring the heat exchanger to divert more warm air into the cockpit without wasting energy?" he asked.

"Yes, it's a question of making best use of the laws of thermodynamics," nodded Grandpa.

"And achieving equivalence in heat distribution to ensure maximum efficiency," Pete added.

Grandpa grinned, his moustache bobbing up and down in agreement.

Jimmy looked from Grandpa to Pete in confusion. This technical talk was making his head spin.

"And in the gadgets department," Grandpa went on, "I was thinking about some kind of hammer, or axe, something to smash through the ice."

"Yeah," growled Pete approvingly. Jimmy thought he saw a glimmer of excitement in the giant mechanic's dark eyes. "A huge hammer. A *massive* hammer. Spring-loaded. Hydraulic retraction. Turbo-charged."

"Now it's funny you should say that," beamed Grandpa. "I'll get us a cup of tea and a chocolate biscuit. When I get back, I'll show you an idea I've been working on…"

Pete nodded. "Sounds good."

Jimmy grinned. He had a feeling those two were going to get on pretty well, after all. Then he tried to stifle a jaw-breaking yawn. It had been a long day.

"Don't worry, Jimmy," said Grandpa from over at the tea-station. Our new friend Pete and I can handle it from here if you want to catch up on your beauty sleep. You've got a long day ahead of you tomorrow."

"OK, then. Goodnight, Grandpa. Goodnight, Pete. 'Night, Cabbie," Jimmy said with another yawn.

"Sleep tight," called Cabbie as Jimmy began to wander off to his cabin. "Don't let the computer bugs bite."

Two minutes later, Jimmy was wrapped up in bed beneath two duvets and a thick blanket, listening to the howling freezing wind outside, battering the airship.

Even though this was going to be his third race, he still couldn't quite believe it. Tomorrow, he, Jimmy

Roberts, would be driving in the Robot Races, across the Arctic circle, with Pete Webber on his team.

Unbelievable, he thought to himself as he drifted off to sleep.

The next morning, Jimmy woke up still dreaming of the upgrade he might get if he won the Arctic race – sonic-boom rocket-boosters to take Cabbie beyond the speed of sound, a robocopter-converter to take Cabbie into the air at the flick of a switch…

Jimmy sat up and yawned. He couldn't wait to see the modifications Grandpa and Pete had made to Cabbie overnight. He threw on his clothes and ran all the way from his cabin to Grandpa's workstation.

He found Grandpa, Cabbie and Pete Webber exactly where he'd left them, surrounded by more empty tea mugs and plates than he could count.

"Morning, Jimmy," yawned Grandpa.

"Hey, Jimmy," said Pete.

"What a night!" called Cabbie. "You wait 'til you see what we've been up to!"

"Show me!" said Jimmy, putting his head in Cabbie's window and examining the control panel. "Hey, Grandpa, what's the orange lever do?"

Grandpa said nothing.

"Grandpa?"

Jimmy turned. Grandpa seemed to have gone to sleep face down in his teacup.

"Your grandpa's had a long night," whispered Pete. "He's some genius, I tell you. It's no wonder you're doing so well in the championship with a man like that on your team."

"And now we're going to do even better with you on the team," whispered Jimmy. "That special upgrade prize is going to be mine for certain!"

"Hey, Wilf," Pete whispered in Grandpa's ear. "Wake up and show your boy what Cabbie's got up his sleeves."

Grandpa's head jerked up, his wild white moustache springing into his eyes. "What's that?" he mumbled. "Yes, what was I saying?"

"You were just telling me about the modifications you and Pete have been working on," smiled Jimmy.

"Ah, yes," said Grandpa, stroking his moustache

back into position and clearing his throat. "Yes, well …
see the orange lever? Pull it and see what happens."

Jimmy tugged on the orange lever. A rhythmic
thumping boomed out, making the whole airship
shake. Cabbie jumped up and down in time with
the pounding beat, and the pit area echoed with
the sound of ripping metal. Jimmy looked around in
horror and realized Grandpa was shouting something
at him.

"Turn it off!" bellowed Grandpa.

Jimmy pushed the orange lever back and the
thumping stopped as suddenly as it had started.

"Wow!" cried Cabbie. "What a mover!"

"Oops," said Grandpa with a sheepish grin.
"I didn't expect it to make quite that much of
a racket."

"That's your robo-pummeller," said Pete Webber.
"A massive, turbo-sprung jackhammer fixed to
Cabbie's underside. It can squash snow to make the
ground smoother, so you'll be able to turn a snowdrift
into an ice road in about three seconds."

"And knock a hole in the floor of an airship in
about two seconds," said Grandpa, looking nervously

around to see if anyone had noticed the damage they had done.

"And then there's the roto-blade," explained Pete. "You push that green button next to the orange lever and a razor-sharp circular saw with huge teeth extends from Cabbie's roof. It's telescopic, can pivot in any direction and will cut through anything – ice, compacted snow, rock, you name it."

"Wow," said Jimmy, leaning in and pressing the button.

Bang!

A huge parachute was fired from Cabbie's roof. It slowly floated down and covered all of them.

"Oops," said Jimmy. "I thought you said it was the green button!"

"Shall I repackage?" came Cabbie's voice through the darkness beneath the parachute.

"Good idea," said Grandpa.

"You need to be careful," said Pete when Cabbie had retracted the parachute and folded it back into his roof. "The *dark green* button releases the parachute. The *light green* button activates the roto-blade."

Jimmy peered at the buttons. "You could have

chosen another colour..." he muttered.

"There's some other things you should know," continued Pete. "I've put my spare toolkit in the trunk – remember there are no pit stops in this race and you may need to do some running repairs while you're out on the ice. I can talk you through anything you're not sure about over the Cabcom."

"And we've put snow tyres on, of course," added Grandpa, "but if it gets really slippy out there you can activate a set of snow chains with that blue button," he said, pointing to it on Cabbie's dashboard. "Press it and they will automatically wrap round Cabbie's tyres. You will probably lose a bit of top-end speed, but what you lose in pace you'll gain in grip."

"That's about it," said Pete. But Jimmy didn't hear him. The mechanic's voice was drowned out by the sound of a warning klaxon booming around the pit area, the creaking groan of the airship's huge steel door being opened and a biting blast of cold air whistling past their ears.

"Drivers, you have just five minutes until the race begins," echoed the voice of Lord Leadpipe. "That's five minutes," he repeated.

Jimmy took a deep breath and smiled at Grandpa and Pete. "This is it," he said, climbing into Cabbie's cockpit.

"Good luck, my boy," said Grandpa, winking and grinning proudly.

Pete gave a nod. "See you at the finish line," he growled, but there was a warm smile on his face.

Jimmy fired up Cabbie's engines and looked out through his windscreen, through the airship door to the Arctic ice beyond. Blinding white, it gleamed in the sunlight, stretching to a brilliant blue sky. It looked like the edge of the world.

Jimmy guided Cabbie down the ramp onto the ice.

Race marshals with flags lined the route to the start line. They waved him forward and into his starting position.

The start line was right next to Lord Leadpipe's igloo. There were no grandstands for this leg of the championship as it was far too cold and dangerous for crowds to gather. But it seemed as if every camerabot in the world had made it instead. The hovering robotic cameras sprayed de-icer onto their lenses to stop their cameras from instantly freezing over.

Jimmy knew that there would be millions of people sat in their living rooms at home, edging closer to the screen and feeling the excitement that only the Robot Races could cause. The idea of all those people watching him made his tummy do a somersault.

Instead of the usual cheering from the crowds, all Jimmy could hear was the howling of the wind as it whipped around the robots and stirred up a blizzard in front of the racers' eyes.

The racers pulled up to the start line: Monster and Missy, Kako and Lightning, Chip and Dug, Sammy and Maximus, and lastly, Horace and Zoom. Each one of the robots looked like they had been freshly painted and polished, with shiny new stickers advertising their sponsors. Even Cabbie had a new *That's Shallot!* sticker on his bonnet. The stupid onion logo was just the same though. The camerabots darted among them, and huge images of each racer appeared on the airship's vast display screens. None of the drivers looked at each other. They were all staring anxiously down the track at what lay ahead.

Lord Leadpipe's track engineers had been busy overnight. They had cut a vast channel in a straight line through the snow and built its banks up, so the track curved up at the edges like a bobsleigh run. It was a half-pipe, a giant U-shape in the distance, reaching all the way to the horizon.

"Racers," Lord Leadpipe's voice boomed from the airship's loudspeakers, "the first ten-kilometre stretch of the race will be a straight sprint down this specially-created track, which I'm calling the Arctic Roll! At the end of the Roll, you'll come to a crossroads. It's left for the snow route, straight on for the ice route, and right for the sea route. The race will begin in ten … nine…"

"Which route are we taking, Jimmy?" asked Cabbie, revving his engines and running some last minute software checks.

Jimmy felt a cold lump spread down his thoat like he'd just swallowed a lump of ice. He, Grandpa and Pete had spent so long talking about Cabbie's improvements that they'd forgotten to choose which route to take!

"Four … three…" echoed the countdown.

"We need to decide, Jimmy," said Cabbie, "cos we're off!"

CHAPTER FIVE
Into the Unknown

"Two … one … GO! GO! *GO!*" cried Lord Leadpipe standing on the top of his igloo, microphone in hand. His voice was almost drowned out by the roar of engines and the howl of the Arctic wind.

All six racers shot away from the start line, skidding and sliding, bouncing over the snow like bumper cars. The ground beneath them screamed as the racers' spinning tyres sprayed chips of ice and sent columns of steam and smoke into the air.

Jimmy gripped the steering wheel, his knuckles turning white. He pulled ahead of Princess Kako, who was struggling to keep her robobike, Lightning, upright while dodging the other racers as they span and skidded towards her. Sammy and Horace also seemed to be having slow starts, but Missy looked less worried about bumps – she was laughing as the other racers jumped and swerved. Missy put her foot down and Monster's enormous bulk tore off into the lead.

"What a mess!" said Jimmy, glancing at the chaos in his rear-view mirror as the churning snow made it difficult to see who was where.

"Never mind them," said Cabbie. "Let's try to stay up front and out of trouble."

Chip and Dug were in hot pursuit of Missy, so Jimmy tucked Cabbie in behind them, using Dug as a buffer against the savage wind.

"Great start, Jimmy," said Cabbie.

"Time to get in the lead," said Jimmy, gritting his teeth and turning the steering wheel to pull out and overtake. Cabbie swerved wildly and started skidding sideways at a terrifying speed.

"What's wrong with the steering, Cabbie?" cried Jimmy anxiously. "What's going on?"

"Aquaplaning!" said Cabbie. "Dug's exhaust is

melting the snow. We're surfing on top of the snow at the moment!"

The steering wheel continued to jerk left and right, and Jimmy felt like he was juggling a bar of soap as it slipped through his fingers.

"Should we activate the snow chains?" asked Cabbie as they careered from side to side.

"Not right now. We just need to get away from Dug's exhaust," decided Jimmy. He took his foot off the accelerator and let Cabbie drop back. With one sharp twitch on the steering wheel, Jimmy managed to guide Cabbie out to the right and onto solid snow. Jimmy stamped on the accelerator.

"I've stabilized wheelspin," said Cabbie, his revs rising as they rocketed forwards. "Now we're motoring!" he cried as they streaked past Dug and into second place.

Looking in his rear-view mirror, Jimmy could see Chip's racer lagging further behind. While the track was like this, the digger-bot's caterpillar tracks weren't as effective as Cabbie's tyres.

"The track's getting narrower," said Jimmy after a few minutes. "Soon there won't be room for overtaking. We need to get around Missy before it's too late—"

Before he could finish, Jimmy saw a flash in his rear-view mirror as Sammy and Maximus shot past Chip. "Looks like Sammy's making the most of his new fan blades. He'll be past us in a second," Jimmy murmured.

"Look how fast Maximus is on this snow," Cabbie said as the hoverbot swept past them and settled smoothly into second place.

Jimmy looked down at his GPS readout on the Cabcom and saw that all six racers were now close together as the snow road narrowed.

"Cabbie, can you find the best route through?" cried Jimmy.

"I'm computing, I'm computing!" said Cabbie.

Just at that moment Jimmy felt a bump as Cabbie hit a pothole in the icy surface of the half-pipe. The jolt made the wheel lock up and Cabbie was sent skidding at a 45-degree angle to the track.

"Whoa!" said Cabbie as slushy snow sprayed out in every direction.

As Cabbie skidded, Jimmy jabbed at the blue

button on his dashboard. There was a metallic clunk and a clacking noise as specially-made chains snaked round the tyres.

"Snow chains engaged," said Cabbie. "We've got control back. Great idea, Jimmy."

"Thanks, Cabbie," Jimmy said with a grin. He eased Cabbie back into a straight line and squeezed the accelerator once more.

They'd lost a few valuable seconds and now Chip and Dug were right on their tails again.

Trapped between Dug and Maximus, Jimmy tried to hold Cabbie steady. As they were squeezed tighter and tighter between the two massive robots, the back of Maximus's inflatable air cushions skimmed Cabbie's front bumper.

"What are they doing?" asked Jimmy.

"Trying to knock us out of the way, I think," said Cabbie cheerily.

"Sammy wouldn't do that!" said Jimmy, desperately hoping he was right.

Sure enough, Sammy's face popped up on the Cabcom screen. "Sorry Jimmy!" he yelled. "This snow is slippery, no?"

Maximus veered towards them again, hitting Cabbie a glancing blow which sent him flying sideways and up the side of the Arctic Roll.

"Strap on your circuit boards!" cried Cabbie as they veered back into the path of Chip and Dug.

With a deafening crack and a blinding flash, Dug suddenly glowed blue.

Jimmy gritted his teeth as Cabbie hit Dug's blue light and was flung away, careering back towards Maximus's vast air cushion.

"What's that?" asked Jimmy.

"An electro-force field," said Cabbie as they sailed towards Maximus.

"I feel like a pinball!" shrieked Cabbie as they bounced between the two towering racers on either side of them.

"And it looks like the track's just about to narrow even more when we get to that bend," Jimmy said, looking at the steep sides to the course. "There's only one thing for it." He stamped on the accelerator again and yanked on the steering wheel. Veering sharply to the left, Cabbie rocketed up the bank of the Arctic Roll half-pipe.

"What are you doing?" cried Cabbie. "I'm the wrong way up!"

"Hold on," Jimmy said calmly. "We're going to keep out of trouble and take the high side of the curve, then we'll slingshot right past the others. Keep your pistons pumping and we'll be fine."

"Gotcha, Jimmy. Full power coming right up."

Cabbie adjusted his settings and the engine roared with more power. Jimmy was thrown back in his seat as they skimmed the very top of the half-pipe. He could feel the G-force squeezing his face and trying to prise his hands off the steering wheel as they hurtled through the bend. For one terrifying moment he thought that the tyres were losing grip and they might topple sideways and roll back down the hill to get crushed under Dug's wheels, but the snow chains bit deep into the high sides of the bend and they held firm. Then Jimmy gave a little twist of the steering wheel and Cabbie arced downwards. Using the slope to pick up extra speed, they shot downhill and flew ahead of both Sammy and Chip.

They were back in second behind Missy and Monster.

Cabbie let out a deafening yodel as they hit the bottom of the slope again. "Amaaaaaaaaaaazing!" he shouted. "Nice thinking, Jimmy ... And excellent work by me, obviously."

Grandpa's face popped up on the Cabcom. He must have had his face pressed right up to the camera – all Jimmy could see was a huge grin and an even bigger moustache. They filled the whole screen.

"That was incredible. Quick thinking, Jimmy lad. Well done!"

"Thanks, Grandpa," said Jimmy.

"And Pete's had a message from Big Al," Grandpa went on. "He says ... what did he say, Pete?"

Jimmy heard Pete mumbling something in the background.

"Big Al says he could learn a thing or two from you!"

"What?" cried Jimmy, veering off course in amazement.

"And I bet I could teach that Crusher a thing or two as well," Cabbie boasted.

"Anyway," Grandpa went on, "the main thing is, you've got about two kilometres until the track splits.

Do you know what route you're going to take?"

"The snow track, I think," replied Jimmy. "At least that way I'll be able to keep an eye on the others."

"You're the boss," said Cabbie. "I'm just as happy crashing through the ice into the sea as I am dropping down a crevasse and never being seen again. I think they're both great ideas."

"Thanks," said Jimmy flatly. "That's really helpful."

"One kilometre until the track splits," came Grandpa's voice again. "It's about to get interesting, my boy!"

As they came towards the last few hundred metres of the Arctic Roll, the gaps between the racers tightened once more. They were jammed together nose to tail as they powered through the half-pipe.

"Breathe in, Cabbie, we're getting squeezed," said Jimmy as the steep walls came dangerously close to taking off Cabbie's wing mirrors.

Behind them, Dug and Maximus were both sending up a flurry of snow as they sped along.

"Hey!" cried Chip over the Cabcom. "This track is ruining my paintwork!"

Up in front, Cabbie could see Monster's huge chassis scraping the frozen walls as well. Jimmy could hear Missy over the radio, shouting encouragement at her racer. "Come on, you lazy lump of dingo dung, it's just a bit of frozen water, just power on through."

"Good point," said Cabbie. "I like her style."

"We've made it to the crossroads. Here we go!" shouted Jimmy as all six racers hurtled out of the half-pipe and onto the open section of the course.

In the distance Jimmy could see snow-covered peaks rising up from the ice to the left, a grey sea speckled with ice floes to the right, and, at its edges, ice cliffs like sharp jagged teeth. Straight ahead, a narrow ice track stretched to the horizon.

"Still want the snow track, Jimmy?" asked Cabbie. "The snow on those mountains looks pretty deep."

"And those clouds look like they're just about ready to dump a whole load more snow," Jimmy agreed.

He paused for a second ... then came to a decision.

"Hold onto your hat, Cabbie. We're taking the ice!"

CHAPTER SIX
Dancing on Ice

"Did you hear that, Grandpa?" Jimmy said, punching a button on the Cabcom.

"I can hear you, my boy. You do whatever your gut says is right," said Grandpa.

"Thanks, Grandpa. Anyway, the ice can't be that thin, can it?"

"Have you got your scarf on?" asked Grandpa.

"Yes," Jimmy sighed. "And my thermal vest."

"Good," said Grandpa. "Now when you get onto the ice, keep it steady. If you go too fast, you'll lose control. And you need to keep an eye out for—"

"Hold on a sec, Grandpa," Jimmy interrupted

as he spotted something ahead. "What's that?" He punched a button on the dashboard and one section of the windscreen zoomed in on the route, as if he was peering through binoculars. The track opened up into an expanse of ice as the wind had picked up and whipped dangerously at each of the racers.

"Markers up ahead," said Cabbie, detecting them on his screen. "Left for the snow route, straight on for the ice route, and right for the sea route."

Sure enough, there lay the faint outlines of a track, and off to the left side there was a sign, which read:

BEWARE

Racers failing to stay within the track markings risk straying onto thin ice. Any robot requiring the assistance of Leadpipe safetybots will be disqualified from the race.

"If we get into trouble we'll be rescued," Jimmy said grimly, "but we'll be out of the race!" He squinted into the distance. Snow was beginning to fall now, but he could see sweeping lines across the ice like the impressions left by ice skaters on a rink – but much wider and deeper. *They must be the track markings*, he thought.

"Hold onto your bobble hats," Jimmy yelled. "Can you get a reading on the ice route, Cabbie? Will it take our weight?"

"Computing," replied Cabbie with a whir of his hard drive. "Looks good," he concluded. "The route marked out is easily thick enough, no dangerous cracks detected. We should be fine."

Jimmy hunched lower over the wheel and peered through the whizzing windscreen wipers at the ice track ahead.

Suddenly Lightning surged up through the pack, using first Dug, then Maximus, then Monster to shelter from the wind. Then the robobike streaked ahead of them all before swinging out to the right and making for the dangers of the Arctic Ocean.

Behind Cabbie, Horace and Zoom were neck and neck with Sammy and Maximus. Horace swung left, straight into Maximus, trying to barge the hoverbot out of the way, but instead his sleek black robot, shaped like a sports car, slapped straight into Maximus's air cushions and was sent spinning away. By the time

Horace had regained control he was a long way back.

"Ha," said Jimmy triumphantly. "Serves him right."

Jimmy looked into his rear-view mirror and caught a flash of yellow and gold as Chip sent Dug roaring off to the left and up towards the snow-covered peaks. Just ahead of them were Missy and Monster.

"Just as I thought, Cabbie. Those two racers are the best-equipped to deal with the tough snow terrain."

"And it looks like they are making short work of things already!" replied Cabbie as Dug and Monster quickly climbed through the deep snowdrifts, scattering an avalanche of white powder behind them.

"Wow, look at Princess Kako go," Jimmy said, turning his attention to the right side of the crossroads where Lightning was sprinting towards the ocean. "I hope she knows what she's doing."

With a final burst of acceleration, Lightning rocketed off the edge, diving through the air towards the sea track, which was marked by bobbing Leadpipe buoys. As he flew, Lightning's wheels folded in and a propeller emerged from somewhere beneath his robobike chassis. By the time he hit the water, Lightning had transformed into a jet ski with Kako perched comfortably on top. The girl in silver simply hunched lower over her racer and skimmed out to sea in a storm of spray. She zipped between the floating rocks of ice, getting further and further into the distance until she disappeared from sight.

Jimmy knew that the viewers watching at home would love that manoeuvre. He hoped one of the camerabots had caught it.

Sammy and Maximus followed Kako and Lightning onto the water, his hoverbot air cushions gliding smoothly off the edge of the ice and onto the water without a bump, his huge turbo-propellers leaving a mist of sea spray behind them.

"Come on, Jimmy. It's time to show these heaps of junk what we've got," Cabbie said, and Jimmy turned his attention back to the ice ahead.

"Get ready, Cabbie. Things are about to get slippy," Jimmy warned. And with that, they raced through an opening between the ice cliffs and onto the ice track.

"Woo-hoo!" cried Cabbie.

"Remember, Cabbie," said Jimmy. "Dug and Monster have gone up onto the snow track. It's a much shorter route and those two robot racers can shift that snow like a lawnmower shifts grass."

"We'll be faster," said Cabbie confidently, adjusting his suspension balance. "You watch me. Lightning and Maximus might be fast on the water too, but they're no match for us on this ice."

"And it's just us on the ice track," added Jimmy.

"Even better," said Cabbie with satisfaction. "No one to put us off our game."

"No competition," smiled Jimmy. "We're going to—"

Jimmy stopped talking and listened. There was a low rumble coming from somewhere behind them. It was getting louder. Jimmy glanced in his rear-view mirror. Through the falling snow, he could just make out a black shape coming up behind them. As it drew nearer, it got louder and clearer.

"Oh no," groaned Jimmy.

"Horace Pelly and Zoom are right behind us," announced Cabbie. "And they're coming up fast."

CHAPTER SEVEN
Off Ice

"Zoom's gaining on us," said Cabbie grimly.

"What can we do?" asked Jimmy as he steered into a wide, arcing bend in the ice track.

"My sensors reckon I'm at top speed on this ice," said Cabbie. "I'm just about hanging onto it. If we go any faster, I'm not sure I can stay in control. Anything could happen," he warned. "But we could fire the rocket-boosters, I suppose."

"No," replied Jimmy firmly. "This ice is too fragile for that. We'd burn a hole straight through to the ocean. We're going to have to come up with something else."

There was a moment's silence while Jimmy sat and thought. He looked in Cabbie's rear-view mirror again. Zoom filled it. He was right behind them and Jimmy could see the outline of Horace hunched over his steering wheel, his perfect white teeth gritted in concentration. Suddenly Zoom swung away, out of sight. Jimmy switched his attention to the wing mirror.

"They're pulling out to the right," said Cabbie. "They're going for an overtake."

"Are you sure we can't go any faster?" asked Jimmy.

"Not if you want to keep going in a straight line and stay alive," said Cabbie.

"That gives me an idea!" said Jimmy. He jerked the steering wheel to the right. Cabbie veered in front of Zoom, blocking the move.

"Recalculating traction!" screamed Cabbie as they careered across the ice, all four of his wheels spinning and sliding sideways.

"Straight line!" Jimmy grinned. "Good idea, Cabbie. If they can't get past us they can't get ahead!"

Horace didn't dare drive off the track onto the thinner part of the ice sheet. Zoom pulled back to the left and began to accelerate.

"They're going for it again," said Cabbie.

Jimmy jerked the wheel back to the left. Cabbie hurtled back towards the centre of the ice track, blocking Zoom again.

"That's frightened them away!" said Cabbie triumphantly. "They're backing off!"

Jimmy snatched another look in Cabbie's rear-view mirror. Cabbie was right. Zoom had dropped right back.

Cabcom crackled into life and there was Horace Pelly's face filling the screen. "Having trouble steering that old bucket of yours?" sneered Horace.

"Having trouble overtaking us in that tin can of yours?" replied Jimmy smartly.

"Oh, I'll win this race, Jimmy," said Horace. "Don't you worry about that. That super-awesome-Leadpipe-upgrade will be mine. Not that I need it, of course. Whatever the upgrade is, I'll probably have one already – so it'll probably be a *down*grade for me. But I'd still like to win it – just to stop *you* from having it."

Jimmy rolled his eyes and sighed. "Have you nearly finished talking?" he asked.

"Yes … just one last thing," said Horace, grinning slyly. "Remember this face." He pushed his nose into the screen. "Take a good look – because this is the face you'll see at the top of the winners' podium."

"Don't look at his face, Jimmy. It'll make you feel sick," Cabbie laughed.

"How hilarious," said Horace flatly. "We'll see who's laughing at the finish line, shall we, *Scabbie*?"

Cabcom went blank.

"He can't get past us," said Jimmy, nodding confidently. "The track's too narrow here."

"But look ahead," replied Cabbie. "It's opening out again in just a few hundred metres! This section of ice must be much stronger."

Cabbie was right. Soon they were crossing a huge expanse of open ice with the grey sea lapping at its edge.

Zoom soon appeared on Cabbie's right-hand side again. Jimmy glanced over to see Horace Pelly grinning through his window at him, and waving. Then Horace reached down and pressed a button on the dashboard.

"Oh no!" said Jimmy. "I hope he hasn't just—"

With a rush of flame and a huge boom, Horace's rocket-boosters fired and he shot past Jimmy and Cabbie, into the lead.

"We're losing grip, Jimmy," said Cabbie as they skidded left, then right. "Those rockets are turning the ice to water and we're sloshing around with no control at all – our snow chains can't get a hold of the ice."

"I knew using boosters was dangerous," muttered Jimmy. "I'm going to slow down a bit, Cabbie. We need to go carefully until we get past him."

Just at that moment, Cabcom crackled back into life.

"Not you again!" sighed Jimmy.

"Don't be so rude, Jimmy," said Grandpa.

"Oh, sorry, Grandpa," said Jimmy. "I thought you were Horace."

"Been bothering you, has he?" Grandpa grunted. "You need to get back up there and show him, Jimmy lad. Fire the rocket-boosters and you'll storm ahead!"

"No," said Jimmy, "we can't do that. Horace's boosters have just melted the ice. If we fire Cabbie's rocket-boosters too, we could end up breaking the ice and falling into the sea! We're going to have to come up with something else."

"OK, my boy. It's your call," said Grandpa. "I know you'll think of something. You always do."

Cabcom crackled and the screen went blank again.

Jimmy peered ahead at Zoom disappearing into the distance. From underneath Zoom's black chassis there came a strange orange glow. It wasn't his rocket-boosters – they'd done their job and burned out long ago.

"Cabbie, what's going on up ahead?" asked Jimmy urgently as Cabbie fought for grip. The steering wheel was jolting wildly in Jimmy's hands. "Activate zoom screen," said Jimmy, his voice starting to shake as they swerved from side to side.

The zoom screen popped up above the dashboard. It showed Zoom racing ahead, roaring along on a cushion of flame.

"He's using his flame-throwers. And he's pointing them down at the ice!" cried Jimmy. "No wonder we're sliding all over the place."

"It's worse than that," said Cabbie urgently. "My sensors reckon the ice is barely taking our weight. He's not just melting the ice – he's burning through it!"

As Cabbie spoke, an almighty creaking and groaning ripped through the air, making Jimmy's ears ring and his heart stop. A thin black crack opened up in the ice ahead of them – a thin black crack that shot towards them like a fork of lightning, just as violent, just as fast. The crack widened. And then another one opened up. And another.

"The ice is breaking up!" cried Jimmy. We're going to—"

SPLOSH!

Cabbie and Jimmy were tipped into the freezing Arctic sea!

CHAPTER EIGHT
That Sinking Feeling

Jimmy was thrown forwards onto the steering wheel as the world disappeared and the grey ocean rose up and swallowed Cabbie. They dropped like a stone straight down towards the sea bed.

"What do we do? What do we do?" gasped Jimmy.

The faint light through the ice above them was disappearing fast and they were plummeting backwards into blackness. Through the gloom Jimmy could just make out three blinking lights which had suddenly appeared on the surface. *Safetybots*, he thought with a groan.

"Cabbie!" he cried as the engine cut out. "Do

something! If we don't get back to the surface fast, we'll be fished out and disqualified." Already the temperature in Cabbie's cockpit was dropping rapidly as the heaters clogged up with water.

"Oh no. This doesn't look good at all," wailed Cabbie.

"We need to d-d-d-d-do something. But w-w-w-what?" Even in his Hotfoot™ socks and thermal underwear, Jimmy was starting to shiver violently.

The dim light was fading as they sank further into the blackness of the deep ocean. Dark moving shapes loomed through Cabbie's windows and Jimmy couldn't stop himself wondering whether they might be killer whales or giant squid.

"I can't see a thing," said Jimmy. "Have we got emergency lighting? I need to see the dashboard controls."

"My circuits are f-f-freezing up," stammered Cabbie, his voice rising and falling randomly. "And I'm losing my contact light engine in the boo-boo-boo-booster."

"What?" said Jimmy. "What are you talking about?"

"I d-d-d-d-don't know," stuttered Cabbie. "My

communication processor I zip-flippedy hydraulic malfunction skippidy-doodily-dah thermostat is not responding."

"Gotta think. Gotta think," said Jimmy. He felt like his brain was starting to go numb, like when he ate ice cream too quickly...

"Processing sqqquuaaarkkk unstable," said Cabbie, still talking nonsense. "Shut down. Shut down."

Jimmy flicked on the Cabcom. "Grandpa?" he called. "Grandpa, come in." He stared into the blank screen. It was dead. "There must be something we can use to get us back up to the surface," said Jimmy, thinking aloud. "What have we got?" he went on, thinking through all the gadgets that could save them. "Parachute? No. We want to go up not down. Roll cage? No. We're not turning over, we're sinking. EFD? Emergency Flotation Device! That's it!" he shrieked. "We need to float. And this is an emergency for certain. Cabbie, activate the EFD!"

"Act-act-act—" stammered Cabbie.

Nothing happened. Now Jimmy really was on his own. Cabbie's central processor was all over the place and there was no one else to help him. But which button was it? If he got it wrong and released the parachute it would drag them right to the bottom of the sea, far from the reach of any safetybots.

Jimmy gulped. His finger hovered between the many buttons lit up in front of him: red, green, orange, yellow, blue—

"Think, Jimmy, think," he said to himself as red lasers pierced the darkness all around him. The safetybots were scanning, preparing to make an extraction. *The parachute button was light green ... no, no – it was dark green. And the roto-blade was light green. The pummeller was that orange lever ... But what colour was the EFD?* Jimmy thought back to the last time he'd used it, to skim over the quicksand in the jungle. But he'd just yelled at Cabbie to inflate it. Jimmy shook his head. *He had to do something!* He thumped the nearest button and prayed he hadn't made a huge mistake.

Hssssssssss!

With a rush of air, the dingy popped out around Cabbie's sides. Cabbie began to rise through the water in a whirlwind of bubbles. Faster and faster they shot through the water. Jimmy's stomach climbed into his throat and his ears popped like corks as they rocketed to the surface and burst back out into the world in an explosion of water.

When the chaos had calmed, Jimmy peered out of the windscreen. They were bobbing on the sea, like they were floating on a lilo. Above his head, the safetybots hummed like angry bees, three large orbs the size of cannon balls spinning in the air. Then after a moment the red flashing lights on the robots blinked green and with a *whirrrrrr* they zoomed away.

"Are you all right, Cabbie?" asked Jimmy once his head had stopped spinning.

"I think so," croaked Cabbie. "But I'm not getting any warmer floating around like this. I think it's time to stop swimming and get out!"

"Good plan," smiled Jimmy with relief. "But how? Can we pull ourselves out with the grappling hook?"

Jimmy looked around. They were bobbing around at least twenty metres from what looked like a shelf of solid ice.

"I'll give it a go," said Cabbie. "The steel cable's thirty metres long. It'll reach the ice, but I don't know if it will hold on. It could crack the ice." And with that the compartment on his bonnet slid open and the grappling hooks rose, ready to launch. "Identifying target," said Cabbie, his computer scanning the ice shelf for a spot that would take their weight. With a beep, Cabbie zeroed in on the best option.

"*Fire!*"

The hooks flew through the air and sank into the ice with a dull thud.

"It sounds pretty solid," said Jimmy. "Reel it in, Cabbie."

"Slowly..." said Cabbie, activating the motorized winch and reeling in the steel cable. "Slowly..."

The cable went taut, and for a second Jimmy thought it had done its job. But then the grappling hook tore away from the ice sheet and came hurtling back towards them with a rattle and a clank as it skipped over the hard surface.

"It's not holding!" cried Jimmy.

Then the hook suddenly caught again – and this time it bit deep and held firm. Cabbie tested his weight on it with a sharp tug.

"It's good!" he cried. "Let's go."

The whirring motor on Cabbie's winch began to

reel in the steel cable, pulling them through the water towards the ice. Jimmy's teeth were gritted and he was grinding them every centimetre of the way.

In less than a minute the cable had pulled them through the freezing water to the edge of the ice shelf.

"Go slowly, Cabbie," said Jimmy. "We don't want to go through the ice again and end up back where we started."

Cabbie's winch motor slowed to a low rumble. Centimetre by centimetre, the taut steel cable pulled Cabbie's front bumper onto the ice, then his front wheels, then his back wheels. Beneath the robot's tyres there came a creaking and a groaning noise. But the ice stayed in one piece.

Finally they were perched on the ice, sea water pouring out of Cabbie's every crack.

Jimmy sat for a moment, listening to the worrying sounds of the ice beneath them. Cabbie, meanwhile, retracted the EFD and tucked it back into its storage compartment under his chassis.

"Let's get going!" said Cabbie enthusiastically. "Don't forget, we've got a race to win!"

"You're definitely feeling better," laughed Jimmy.

"I'm like a rubber ball," said Cabbie. "I bounce back from anything!" He revved his engines, coughing and spluttering the sea water out of his pipes. "Ready?" he said.

"Ready," said Jimmy. He flicked Cabbie into first gear and crushed the accelerator pedal with his foot. They were off, roaring back to the ice track and getting back in the race.

"Run a check on all your functions, Cabbie," said Jimmy as they sailed over the ice, rising to top speed.

"I'm already on it," said Cabbie. "I'm fully rebooted and starting self-repair now. But we'd better not end up in the water again," he added. "The air canister for the EFD's empty so we can't use it any more."

"Horace could have done us some real damage back there," said Jimmy angrily.

"I told you, Jimmy, I'm fine," said Cabbie cheerily.

"But after all the hard work Grandpa and Pete put into you, Horace has to go and pull a stunt like that." Jimmy sighed, shaking his head, "He doesn't care what happens to anyone else as long as he's OK. What an idiot!"

"Speaking of your grandpa, let's tell him we're okay." Cabbie suggested.

"Good idea!" Jimmy agreed. "Fire up Cabcom."

"Oh," said Cabbie anxiously.

"What's up?" asked Jimmy.

"No problem," said Cabbie. "Cabcom's frozen solid so we're out of contact with the team."

"Can you defrost it?" asked Jimmy.

"I'm trying my best, but it might take a while," said Cabbie.

"OK," said Jimmy. "Time to get even with Horace."

"Get even?" repeated Cabbie in surprise.

"Level, I mean," said Jimmy quickly. *And* then *get even!* he thought to himself. *I'm going to teach Horace Pelly a lesson he won't forget!*

CHAPTER NINE
Icebreaker

"How are you doing, Cabbie?" asked Jimmy a little while later. "Have you warmed up?"

"Heading for optimum temperature and speed," said Cabbie. "Getting warmer … even warmer … we're red-hot and racing!"

Cabbie's tyres ate up the ground, his engines roaring loud and clear once more. The ice stretched in every direction, flat and smooth and white and empty.

"We must be miles behind Horace," sighed Jimmy. "And without Cabcom we've got no idea how far ahead he's got."

"Oh!" said Cabbie. "I've got a surprise."

A panel slid back on Cabbie's dashboard. A circle of green glass appeared. It lit up and a line of green light swept round the circle like the minute hand on a watch. Every time the line swept over a little green blob, the machine went 'ping!'

"What is it?" asked Jimmy.

"Pete installed it last night," explained Cabbie. "It's called a radar. They used to use it in the olden days. Grandpa knows all about them, anyway."

"Why have we got it? What does it do?" asked Jimmy.

"See that little green blob?" said Cabbie. "That's Horace."

"Ping!" announced the radar.

"Really?" exclaimed Jimmy. "It's pretty good for an antique, isn't it?"

"Pete said Crusher's coms system is always going down. Big Al uses radar all the time. He says it's basic but more reliable. Big Al loves his radar, Pete says. With this we'll be able to locate any robot within a ten-kilometre radius."

"So how far ahead is Horace?"

"Three kilometres," said Cabbie. "But we're

gaining on him."

Jimmy peered at the radar. The little green blob was getting nearer – but peering through Cabbie's windscreen Jimmy could still see no sign of Horace and Zoom.

A thin flutter of snow landed on the windscreen.

"Weather warning," announced Cabbie. "There's a snowstorm coming in from the north."

Already the flakes of snow had thickened, flying at Cabbie's windscreen as he raced into the storm, splatting on it in big white blotches.

"Activate screen clearance," said Jimmy.

Cabbie set his windscreen wipers flicking and hot air blasting inside, but the snow was flying thicker and faster than he could clear it. It began to creep up the windscreen. Jimmy hunched over the steering wheel and pushed his face to the glass. All he could see was a solid white curtain of flakes flying at him.

"We're going to have to slow down, Cabbie," said Jimmy. "This is dangerous." He eased his foot off the accelerator, and little by little the green blob on the radar moved further and further away from them.

"Horace and Zoom are getting away!" said Cabbie

anxiously. "We'll never catch them if we crawl along like this."

"We'll never catch them if we drop off the ice or fall down a hole because we can't see where we're going!" said Jimmy.

"There must be something we can do," grumbled Cabbie.

"Hold on," said Jimmy. "I've got it!"

"What are you going to do?"

"You know your engine-cooling system?" asked Jimmy.

"Yes," said Cabbie.

"It sucks in cold air, doesn't it?" Jimmy asked excitedly

"That's right," said Cabbie.

"Cabbie, can you reverse it and spray out hot air instead?"

"Consider it done," said Cabbie.

Just like when he was using the grappling hook, the compartment in Cabbie's bonnet slid open. But it wasn't the grappling-hook launcher that rose. It was a huge pipe, like a vacuum cleaner, pointing out into the wall of flying snow.

"Activating snow clearance," announced Cabbie with ice-cool calm.

All of a sudden a large round hole appeared in the snowstorm: a tunnel through the blizzard of snowflakes. The snowstorm raged around them but for at least five metres in front of the car it was crystal-clear.

"It works!" cried Cabbie in amazement.

"Great," said Jimmy.

"Genius!" said Cabbie. "Now, let's get moving. We've got a race to win!"

Jimmy slammed his foot on the accelerator again and pinned his eyes to the tunnel through the snowstorm.

"I can just about see where we're going," he said, "but I can't see if we're going the right way. You might have to navigate for me so I don't steer us back into the sea."

"Our GPS stopped working properly in the storm," Cabbie replied. "We could end up racing back to the start line if we're not careful."

"What about the radar?" asked Jimmy.

"It can help us track Horace," Cabbie said. "But it

can't show us the route."

"Well, let's follow Horace!" Jimmy grinned. "He can actually help us for once!"

"Got it," Cabbie replied, revving his engine.

It took a while, but soon they were out of the storm. And up ahead of them, Jimmy could just make out a distant black blur.

"It's Horace and Zoom," he said. "And they're swerving all over the place!"

"Looks like that snow has caused them a few technical problems," laughed Cabbie.

"We're going to catch them up," said Jimmy as they raced towards Horace, who was still veering from one side of the track to the other.

Jimmy roared up behind them. As he and Cabbie got closer they could see Horace thumping Zoom's steering wheel and shouting and flicking switches furiously.

But just as they were about to pull level and overtake, a huge cloud of snow exploded like an enormous sneeze from somewhere underneath Zoom and he seemed to pull himself together.

Vrmmm! Vrmmm! Zoom's engine let out a deep,

powerful growl and then off he went again.

"He's got the snow out of his system," said Cabbie, "and he's back on track."

"And we're back in the race," said Jimmy. "But I wish we could get him back for melting the ice and putting us in danger," he added angrily.

Jimmy was sick of seeing Horace Pelly playing dirty tricks in the Robot Races championship. For once he wanted to give him a taste of his own medicine.

"That's it!" he cried. "The robo-pummeller. If we can just get ahead by thirty, maybe fifty metres, we can use it to crack a huge hole in the ice. Horace will be falling down it before he even knows it's there. The only place Horace will be racing is to the bottom of the sea!"

"Jimmy?" said Cabbie desperately. "Jimmy, are you there?"

"Of course I am," said Jimmy.

"I thought you must have got out and some idiot taken your place," said Cabbie.

"What do you mean?" asked Jimmy in surprise.

"We can't send Horace down a hole in the ice!" cried Cabbie. "That's exactly what he did to us! It'd make us just as bad as him."

"No we won't," said Jimmy fiercely. "We'd just be paying him back. He started it."

"And besides," said Cabbie, "the robo-pummeller's for getting us through snowy roads, not for smashing through the ice and sending people to the bottom of the sea – even if it is smelly Horace Pelly."

"Listen, Cabbie," said Jimmy. "If we can take Horace out of the race, we'll win for sure. And that robo-upgrade will be ours! Big Al wouldn't think twice about it. He'd be knocking a hole in the ice faster than Pete Webber can change a tyre!"

"Yes, but—"

"Activating rocket-boosters," said Jimmy, stabbing a finger at a button.

A flash of flame sent them rocketing past Horace and skidding over the ice.

"Activating robo-pummeller," said Jimmy, pulling the orange lever forward.

"JIMMY—" Cabbie yelled as he hopped across the ice, jumping up and down like a kangaroo, the robo-pummeller thumping and banging holes in the ice as they went.

In his rear-view mirror, Jimmy grinned as he saw thick black cracks ripping through the ice, rocketing towards Zoom like lightning bolts.

"Jimmy!" Cabbie yelled frantically. "What have you done?"

CHAPTER TEN
Backfire

"Look!" cried Jimmy, glancing in Cabbie's rear-view mirror. Zoom was bumping and bouncing over the jigsaw of breaking ice like a bucking bronco trying to shake off its rider.

The sound of cracking ice rang around the ice cliffs like ricocheting gunfire. The cracks widened into chasms filled with sea water. Steam poured from Zoom's boot as he went into a total spin, hurtling away from Cabbie in widening circles and careering towards a vast hole in the ice.

Jimmy swallowed hard as he watched Zoom reach the very edge of the ice, about to plunge into the freezing water – but with an almighty roar of Zoom's engine, Horace regained control and managed to pull back from the brink, steering his robot towards safer ground.

Jimmy suddenly felt a little uncomfortable. Thinking about teaching Horace a lesson was one thing, but doing it was quite another. He forced down the guilt which was building inside him and pressed the accelerator harder. In Cabbie's rear-view mirror the image of Horace and Zoom got smaller and smaller until they were out of sight.

Jimmy glanced at the radar screen. He could see the green blip that was Horace and Zoom. Around the edge of the screen, four other moving blips had appeared. Jimmy realized it was the other robots. They must be getting near the point where the tracks all met and the racers joined up again. The final stretch before the finish line!

"We're getting close to the end of the ice track, I think," said Jimmy. "And we've left Horace way behind!"

"Oh, good," said Cabbie flatly. "And all we had to do," he added, "was cheat. So that's great, isn't it?"

"What do you mean?" said Jimmy, defensively. "I only did what any of the other racers would have done. And Big Al would *definitely* have done it," he added.

"Would he?" Cabbie asked. "Have you ever seen him pull a stunt like that? And even if he would do it, the Jimmy Roberts I know wouldn't."

Jimmy said nothing. He stared grimly at the ice ahead and chewed angrily at his bottom lip. He glanced at Cabbie's rear-view mirror, half hoping to see Horace racing up behind them. *I might even let Horace overtake,* Jimmy thought to himself, it would make him feel better about what he'd done. There was still no sign of Horace in the mirror – but there was something shooting towards them.

In horror, Jimmy suddenly realized what it was. The cracks in the ice which Jimmy had started with the robo-pummeller were still spreading, and fast, chasing Cabbie across the white surface like giant snakes.

"Cabbie, the ice—" he screamed.

But it was too late. All around him, the ice began to crack.

"Hold on!" Jimmy shouted, veering left then right,

then left again, trying to make his way across the collapsing ice. Each way he turned, the ice ahead of them simply disappeared and the freezing sea welled up in its place. In front, another fracture appeared in the slippery white surface and Jimmy had to hammer the brakes, screeching to a halt.

In stunned silence, Jimmy looked around him at the chaos he had created. For hundreds of metres in almost every direction, chunks of broken ice bobbed in the churning Arctic Ocean. He and Cabbie were perched on a narrow stretch of ice, like a finger pointing out from the solid ice shelf.

"Phew!" said Jimmy, getting his breath back. "That was a close one. Now we're back on solid ground—"

"Solid ice," corrected Cabbie.

"—we can get going again," finished Jimmy.

Cabbie's engines roared into life once more – but they sounded very strange. It was his normal engine noise but with a terrific creaking and groaning added.

"What is it?" asked Jimmy. "What's wrong?"

In dismay, Jimmy realized what was happening. The noise wasn't from Cabbie's engines. It was the ice underneath them!

The creaking and groaning became an ear-splitting screech as the finger of ice they were on broke away from the main ice shelf.

"Quick, Cabbie!" he cried. "We have to jump it!"

But it was too late – all they could do was sit and watch as they began to bob gently out into the Arctic Ocean.

CHAPTER ELEVEN
All at Sea

For almost a minute Jimmy sat perfectly still and silent. The only sound was of water lapping against the ice slab on which Cabbie was floating. He looked back at the ice sheet they had left behind, and then stared out to sea. It stretched for miles and miles, all the way to the horizon and the grey sky – and they were drifting towards the horizon.

Jimmy heard the whine of an engine in the distance. It grew louder – a humming like the noise made by a hive full of bees. Round a corner of the rapidly disappearing coastline came Princess Kako on Lightning, bouncing across the waves on her robobike-turned-jet-ski. She weaved between the icebergs, throwing her bodyweight from side to side expertly as she raced on by.

With a jolt, Jimmy realised they must have floated into the sea track of the race! He hopped out of Cabbie and ran to the edge of the iceberg.

"Hey, Kako! Kako! Hey!" he shouted. "Help!"

She didn't hear him. She didn't see him. Jimmy watched in dismay as the foaming trail she had left behind her was washed away by the waves and she disappeared beyond the ice cliffs.

A couple of seconds later, the vast hoverbot Maximus, piloted by Sammy, came roaring round the same corner in hot pursuit. His dual air cushions glided effortlessly across the sea. His enormous propellers sent up waves, rocking the floating ice island.

Jimmy waved and jumped and shouted – and came to a standstill as Sammy followed Kako and was gone. "Argh!" he yelled in frustration, stamping his foot on the hard white surface beneath his snow boot. Then he climbed back on board Cabbie and sank into his seat. "So," he said. "What do we do?"

Cabbie said nothing.

"Cabbie?" Jimmy asked.

Silence.

Jimmy pressed Cabbie's engine starter. His engine leaped into life.

"Cabbie?" Jimmy tried again. "Cabbie?"

Nothing.

Panic made Jimmy's stomach churn. *Cabbie must have got damaged somehow.*

"Say something, Cabbie!" he said, pushing another button.

Cabbie's chassis lifted about ten centimetres off its wheels on robo-stilts – but still he was silent. Jimmy pressed the button again and Cabbie sank back down – but still Cabbie didn't say a word.

With the panic rushing up from his stomach to his throat, Jimmy pressed another button. Then another button. And another. Nothing worked.

Then suddenly the robot was back in action. Before Jimmy could do anything to stop him, Cabbie threw himself into a doughnut – spinning in incredibly fast and tight little circles, flying around the ice slab with his emergency siren blaring. In panic, Jimmy stabbed at another button. It made Cabbie go even faster. He pressed it again. Cabbie went faster still. He pushed it once more, harder this time. Cabbie's doors started slamming open and shut, open and shut again.

"Agh!" Jimmy cried.

Cabbie's doors flapped wildly. Then he was off again, reversing to the very edge of the ice slab, closer and closer to the water. Jimmy grabbed the steering wheel and yanked it straight.

"Brake!" yelped Cabbie. Without thinking, Jimmy stamped on the brake pedal and they skidded to a standstill. Jimmy jumped out of Cabbie as though the driver's seat was burning him. They were perched on the very edge of the ice slab with freezing sea water lapping at Cabbie's front tyres. Another centimetre and they would have been heading down to the bottom of the sea again.

"Cabbie?" cried Jimmy. "Are you OK? What happened? Did you malfunction?"

"I don't have to talk all the time," said Cabbie quietly. "Just because I don't feel like having a chat, there's no need to start prodding and pressing every button you can see."

"*Don't feel like having a chat?*" repeated Jimmy in

astonishment. "I thought you were *broken*!"

"Well, maybe I don't feel like talking when you've stopped listening," said Cabbie angrily. "It's a waste of my exhaust fumes – especially when your decisions leave us floating around the Arctic on a giant ice cube."

Jimmy looked at the robot, open-mouthed. A feeling of shame was slowly burning through him, making him want to run away and hide. He knew Grandpa wouldn't be proud of him for trying to sabotage another racer. And now even Cabbie didn't want to know him.

He took a deep breath. "Cabbie, I'm so sorry. I was being a complete idiot and I should have listened to you."

"I know," said Cabbie.

"And I promise," said Jimmy, "not to ignore you from now on."

"Good," said Cabbie.

"So do you forgive me? Are we friends again?"

Cabbie said nothing.

"Please?" said Jimmy.

"Of course," said Cabbie. "Apology accepted."

Jimmy grinned in relief.

"So how do we get off this ice cube and back in the race?" Cabbie continued. "We need a plan."

"OK," said Jimmy. "We could..." He paused. Ten seconds passed and still he couldn't think of a good idea. Ten seconds turned to twenty seconds. Then he said, "I know! I'll give you a quick tune-up."

"How's that going to get us back on dry land?" Cabbie asked.

"It's not," Jimmy replied, "but I might as well do something useful while I'm thinking of a way to get off this icicle and back in the race."

"Good idea," said Cabbie, "and I think I might have a quick reboot and self-repair. My sensors are feeling a bit scrambled. I'll go quiet for a minute, but I'll be back before you know it – so don't push any more buttons."

Jimmy hurried to Cabbie's boot and got out the toolkit that Pete Webber had lent him. Also in the boot was a fruit and veg box from *That's Shallot!* that he'd completely forgotten about. The contents were now frozen solid, but that didn't stop him from popping a couple of raspberries into his mouth – they tasted just like fruity ice lollies.

Jimmy had a quick look under the bonnet and cleaned Cabbie's firing mechanism, checked his coolant, oil and brake fluid, and tightened his tyre bolts. By the time he had finished, Cabbie had rebooted.

"Ahhh," sighed Cabbie, "that's *much* better. Everything's peachy and I've even managed to get Cabcom back online. Got a plan yet?"

"Not exactly," said Jimmy.

"Not exactly? Or not at all?" asked Cabbie.

Jimmy sighed in frustration. "If only you could turn into a jet ski like Lightning," he grumbled.

"Well," snapped Cabbie, "I'm *so* sorry to let you down."

"Or if you had a propeller like Maximus does, we could—"

Jimmy stopped talking. His mood lifted as he had a sudden thought.

"What?" said Cabbie. "What is it?"

"The propeller thing!" cried Jimmy.

"What propeller thing?" asked Cabbie.

"Your propeller thing!" said Jimmy.

"I haven't got a propeller thing," said Cabbie.

"No, the thing Pete put in," explained Jimmy excitedly. "Spins round ... cuts through stuff. You know!"

"Do you mean the roto-blade?" asked Cabbie.

"That's it!" said Jimmy. "Cabbie, we're going to turn this ice cube into a power boat!"

CHAPTER TWELVE
Sailing Through

"I hope no one can see us," muttered Cabbie. "This is *so* embarrassing."

Cabbie was parked with his boot open at the very edge of the ice slab. He had extended the roto-blade on its long steel arm, and with a little help from a spanner taken from Pete Webber's toolkit, Jimmy had managed to adjust the angle of the arm and bend it downwards so that the blade and its long razor-sharp teeth were under the water.

From a distance came a whirring like a swarm of flies. Out of the grey cloud flew two of the camerabots that filmed the races for television. As they got nearer, they slowed and hovered, one directly overhead, the other a little further away.

"Great," muttered Cabbie. "How many people are watching us live on TV while I've got my bum in the air?"

"Millions," said Jimmy, trying not to laugh. "So we'd better make sure this works."

"No pressure then," muttered Cabbie.

"Ready?" asked Jimmy. He jumped into Cabbie's cockpit and pushed the roto-blade button. Its motor sprang into life, and from beneath the water came the whir of the blade and a rush of froth and bubbles.

"Are we moving?" called Jimmy.

"Yes!" cried Cabbie. "Yes! We're moving!" And then he went a bit quiet. "Sensors indicate our current speed is approximately ... three kilometres an hour. Travelling at this speed, we should complete the race a week on Tuesday."

"It's working!" said Jimmy. "But not well enough. Adjust the angle on the blade, Cabbie."

Cabbie lifted the roto-blade out of the water, lengthened the arm a little and lowered it back into the water.

"How's that?" he asked.

"I think we're going faster!" cried Jimmy.

"Six kilometres an hour," said Cabbie. "No! Ten ... fifteen ... twenty! Twenty-five kilometres an hour and rising!"

Jimmy cheered. "It works!" he shouted. "It works brilliantly!"

Little by little they picked up more speed, and soon they were cruising smoothly between the chunks of floating ice and heading back towards the ice shelf. Jimmy stood by Cabbie's side with one arm draped affectionately across Cabbie's bonnet and both eyes firmly trained on the ice shelf.

"Left a bit ... right a bit," Jimmy called. "Can we go any faster?"

"Hang on," said Cabbie, increasing the revs on the roto-blade. "How's that?"

With a surge and a wash of foam and spray, the ice-boat shot forward.

"This is incredible!" shouted Jimmy. "We should have done this sooner!"

"I hope those camerabots are getting some good shots," said Cabbie.

"Can you get Robo TV working again so we can have a look?" said Jimmy.

"I'll have a go," replied the robot. "The electronics should all be dry and warm again."

There was a clicking noise and then the screen on Cabcom flickered into life.

"...something we've never seen before in the history of Robot Races," one of the TV commentators was saying. "Incredible!" The pictures showed an aerial shot of Cabbie and Jimmy racing over the waves leaving a trail of foam behind them. Jimmy looked up and waved at the camerabot. "And hi to you too, Jimmy Roberts," said the commentator, chuckling to himself.

"There's no time for waving at the cameras," came Grandpa's voice – his face popping up on the Cabcom screen too. "You're coming up to the crossroads where the three tracks join up again. The track gets pretty narrow after it, so whoever gets there first has a massive advantage. Me and Pete were wondering where you'd got to," he added, "but I love the speedboat. Great thinking, Jimmy lad!" His eyes twinkled and his moustache bobbed up and down.

"Go, Jimmy, go!" he shouted and the screen went blank.

Jimmy smiled proudly to himself. But not for long, as a familiar black shape sped past on the ice track. Horace and Zoom had overtaken them again.

"No time to worry about them now," said Cabbie. "It's time to get back on the ice." He adjusted the roto-blade and steered them towards the ice shelf.

They were heading for the solid ice at an alarming speed – but not fast enough.

Jimmy realized they needed to time their landing perfectly if they were going to avoid getting wet for the second time that day.

"OK," he said, trying not to sound worried. "Retract roto-blade, Cabbie. We want to glide off this ice cube and back onto the ice shelf. If we hit it too hard, we'll smash the ice and end up at the bottom of the sea."

The ice shelf got nearer. From the water, the ice looked incredibly thick – like a huge step they were about to collide with. It was going to be a bumpy ride.

"Ready to go?" asked Jimmy.

"Ready," said Cabbie. "Get in, Jimmy, and get your driving head on!"

Jimmy climbed into Cabbie's cockpit. As they neared the ice shelf, Cabbie's engine roared and Jimmy's foot hovered over the accelerator.

"Three metres," said Cabbie in quiet concentration. "Two metres..." Jimmy put Cabbie into gear. "One metre ... Go! GO! *GO!*"

Jimmy slammed his foot on the pedal just as they hit the ice shelf with a terrific thump.

In a cloud of smoke, Cabbie flew off the ice raft and hit the ice with a massive, bone-shaking, brain-rattling *thud*. In one smooth sweep of the wheel Jimmy guided Cabbie back onto the racetrack and headed for the crossroads where all three routes joined once more.

"Brilliant!" said Cabbie.

"Not bad," agreed Jimmy with a modest smile.

"Jimmy!" called Cabbie. "Look at the radar."

Jimmy looked.

The radar's green glowing line swept round the screen, but where there had earlier been five blinking dots, now there was just one big blob.

"Who is it?" he asked. "Has the radar gone haywire?"

"I don't know," said Cabbie. "My navigation says

we're on track and my sensors show all of the other racers are nearby."

"What does it mean?"

"I don't know," said Cabbie.

They could make out a deep rumbling sound like the noise an aeroplane made at take-off. And then, as they rounded a bend in the track they saw a sight that made Jimmy gasp. "Cabbie, look!"

The track up ahead followed the shape of the coastline, with the ocean on the left and a cliff face towering over it on the right – a monstrous snow-capped glacier. Part of the snow cliff had broken away and fallen onto the track! As they watched, more snow came tumbling and bouncing off the jagged hillside. Tonne upon tonne came cascading down like a frosty waterfall.

After a few seconds, the avalanche eased and the rumbling of falling snow faded to an echo. As the powdery fog cleared, Jimmy could just make out five shapes sticking out of the snow like wafers in a huge ice cream. It was the other racers, in a massive icy pile-up!

CHAPTER THIRTEEN
Pile-up

As Jimmy carefully drove Cabbie closer, he realized what had happened. Missy must have grazed the sides of the glacier with Monster's huge tyres and caused the avalanche. Now Monster was almost completely buried in deep, deep snow. Backed up behind Monster was Dug. At least, Jimmy thought it was Dug, but all he could see was a digger arm poking out of a mountain of fallen snow. Dug was followed by Maximus, Lightning and Zoom. They'd all been almost completely buried and they were stuck fast.

It was chaos.

"This is our chance." Cabbie said excitedly. "We

just need to get past them and we'll be on that winner's podium for sure!"

"But how are we going to get through?" Jimmy asked.

"The robo-pummeller," Cabbie replied without hesitation. "It looks like there's a way through down the left-hand side of the pile-up, but we'll need to compact that snow so that I don't get stuck like the rest of them. And we don't want to slip and fall back into the sea. I've had enough of that for one day."

"Right," Jimmy said. "That special prize has got our name on it—"

But before Jimmy could finish speaking there was another grumbling and the cliff face above the robots began to moan. Jimmy could see it slowly shifting as if it were trying to tell the racers that it didn't appreciate having visitors.

"That doesn't sound good," Jimmy said. "Look at that!" Jimmy pointed to the top of the cliff where a big crack was appearing in the cliff face.

It wasn't snow coming loose now – it was a giant block of ice!

"That's got to be as big as a house," Jimmy said,

biting his lip. "If that comes down it'll squash them all like a pancake! Cabbie, we've got to do something!"

"But I thought you would do anything to win?" Cabbie said. "What does it matter what happens to them as long as we beat them? Besides, the safetybots will be along soon enough. Let's go!"

Jimmy stomped on the brakes. "I've learnt my lesson, Cabbie. It's not worth winning if you have to hurt everyone else to do it. I'm not Horace Pelly."

Cabbie's headlights blinked happily. "Well said, Jimmy lad."

There was a flash of orange from deep within the snowdrift, followed by yet more groaning from the cliff face.

"Horace is trying to burn his way out with that flame-thrower of his," said Cabbie. "That kind of heat will make the cliff even less stable."

Just at that moment a new face appeared on the Cabcom. It was Lord Leadpipe. The multi-billionaire's face was pale and he looked like he'd seen a ghost. "Calling all racers, calling all racers," he said. "We're having a ... um ... ah ... slight technical hitch with the safetybots. It appears there's been a malfunction with their de-icers, so they've all frozen solid." He coughed nervously, and then tried to put a smile on his face. It looked more like a grimace to Jimmy. "If you children could, um, keep out of trouble while we sort the problem, then I'll have them up and running in just a jiffy." And with that his face disappeared and the screen went blank once again.

"No one's coming to the rescue," Jimmy gasped. "We've got to do something!"

"Aye, aye, Captain!" Cabbie said, revving his engine.

"Can you turn on Cabcom?" said Jimmy. "I need to talk to everyone."

Cabcom crackled into life.

"Did you hear Lord Leadpipe?" asked Jimmy. "The safetybots aren't coming. It's up to us to get out of this. But everyone needs to help. OK?"

Horace's face popped up on the screen. "I suppose you can't make things any worse," he said with a sneer.

Jimmy ignored him. "I'm going to dig you all out using my roto-blade, but everyone will have to be very careful. There's a big slab of ice coming loose at the top of the cliff and any loud noises or sudden movements might cause an avalanche."

"Thanks, Jimmy," said Kako.

"Great," said Sammy.

"We're relying on ya, buddy," said Chip.

"Cheers, mate!" bellowed Missy.

"Well, get on with it then," said Horace.

The screen went blank again.

"Activate roto-blade?" said Cabbie.

"Yeah, but easy does it, Cabbie," said Jimmy.

Cabbie extended the roto-blade on its long steel arm. Like a dentist performing surgery on a tooth, they carefully cut through the white snow. Jimmy edged Cabbie forward centimetre by centimetre, his nerves jangling as he listened carefully for any sound of another avalanche.

It took just a couple of minutes to get Horace free. In a shower of white dust, the metal blades cut into the snowdrift, scattering it into the Arctic wind.

"Careful of Zoom's paintwork," came Horace's voice from the Cabcom. "If you damage it, you'll have to pay."

"I think you mean 'thank you for rescuing us'!" Cabbie snapped.

"Right, Horace," began Jimmy, "I need you to help me get Lightning and Maximus free now. Can you just—"

Jimmy didn't get a chance to finish. Horace had fired up Zoom's engines and was revving them loudly.

"Horace, what are you doing?" shouted Jimmy into Cabcom.

Horace didn't reply. He was too busy activating Zoom's rocket-boosters. Before anyone could say anything, huge tongues of fire shot from Zoom's exhaust. He shot up the snowdrift where the others were trapped and skated over the top.

"Ha!" Horace yelled triumphantly as he and Zoom landed safely on the other side. "Later, losers." And without another word he disappeared in the direction of the finish line.

A second or two passed while Jimmy stared open-mouthed at the black screen. He couldn't believe what Horace had just done. "What an idiot!" he said.

"Yup," said Cabbie.

Cabcom leaped back into life and Missy's face appeared, looking red and anxious.

"I don't want to worry you guys," she whispered,

"but the ice up where I am is making some pretty strange noises. I think Horace and his rocket-boosters have done it some damage and—"

A deep cracking sound in the ice above them cut Missy off. Jimmy glanced out of Cabbie's window. A huge crack was spreading way above their heads, and lumps of ice and snow began to rain down on them. A second cracking sound rang out and the ice cliff juddered. As the ice shifted, a chunk the size of a car broke off and fell towards the remaining racers.

Jimmy looked at it in horror. The sky went dark as the ice block's shadow fell across them.

BOOM!

The slab hit the track and exploded into a million pieces, no more than a metre from where the Japanese princess and Lightning were half-buried. Shards of ice were fired in every direction, peppering the bodywork of the robots…

Then there was silence.

Jimmy let out a long, slow breath. "That was close," he whispered.

"Yep," Cabbie agreed. "And the rest could come down on us all at any minute!"

CHAPTER FOURTEEN
Cliffhanger

Jimmy and Cabbie had just finished chipping away the last of the snow surrounding Kako and Lightning when a light started flashing on Cabcom.

"There's a message coming through from Chip," said Cabbie.

Jimmy flicked a switch and Chip's face filled the screen. "Calling all racers," he whispered. "I don't know about the rest of y'all, but I wanna get out of this mess right about now."

There was a muttering of agreement from the others. They were all a bit shaken up by the explosion.

Jimmy sat in complete silence for a few seconds.

"We need a better plan," he whispered finally to Cabbie. "What do you think?"

"Well," said Cabbie, "we could race up the snowdrift, over the tops of Dug and Missy and head for the finish line…"

"Like Horace did?"

"Yup," said Cabbie. "Or we could stay here and help the others get out of this mess."

"We've got to stay and help," Jimmy said firmly. "And there's no time to lose," he continued as another shower of ice rained down on them from the glacier. Jimmy leaned into the Cabcom. "Sammy, I'm using my roto-blade to clear the snow around you next. OK?"

"No, Jimmy, not OK," Sammy replied, his anxious face staring out from the Cabcom screen. "Your blades will puncture my air cushions for certain. Maximus will be stuck here and we'll be blocking everyone else in. I am thinking we must try a different way."

"Right," said Jimmy. "Cabbie, switch all systems to manual. I'm taking over."

"What?" said Cabbie.

"I'm taking responsibility for this," said Jimmy,

"so if it all goes wrong, it's my fault."

"OK, Jimmy lad," Cabbie said. "You've listened to me, now I'll listen to you. We're a team. But be careful," he added nervously.

Jimmy pressed a button on the steering wheel and a compartment on Cabbie's bonnet slid open. Up rose the grappling hooks, the sharpened points glinting in the light. Jimmy prodded another button and the angle of the grappling hooks lowered by a few degrees.

"A little more," said Jimmy. "And a bit more…"

Cabcom crackled into life. Sammy's face appeared, red and angry. "What are you doing?"he yelled. "You're aiming straight at Maximus! You'll hit him!"

"Trust me, Sammy. I know what I'm doing. Fire!" said Jimmy, pushing the button.

The grappling hook flew at Maximus, missed his rear left propeller by about three centimetres and crashed into the ice cliff. It bounced off and sent a shower of ice chips over Maximus's cab.

"Jimmy, stop right now!" Sammy shouted.

Jimmy leaned over to the screen and turned it off. Then he reeled the grappling hook back in on its thick steel cable. It clattered and clanked over the ice, making its way back to the launcher on Cabbie's bonnet. "I'm reloading and adjusting the angle," he said determinedly. "Five centimetres right."

He paused and took a deep breath.

"Here goes!" He pushed the launch button again. This time the grappling hook flew between Maximus's propellers and wrapped itself around the steel structure on which his propellers were mounted.

"Yes!" shouted Jimmy. "Gotcha. Reel him in, Cabbie. We'll drag Maximus out of the snow, and once he's free he can help us dig the others out."

"Brilliant!" Cabbie cried. "But ... how ... I mean..." he stuttered.

"Has your speech software malfunctioned?" Jimmy laughed. "Just keep your circuits crossed that this works, otherwise we're all in big trouble."

The steel cable of the grappling hooks pulled taut and dragged Cabbie forward, making him slip awkwardly on the ice. Hurriedly, Jimmy turned the winch off.

"We need to anchor ourselves, Cabbie," said Jimmy. "Otherwise we'll end up stuck in there too."

"I've got just the thing," replied the robot. "You aren't the only one with a few tricks up his sleeve valve."

Clunk!

Two sharpened pieces of metal, shaped like skewers, thudded into the ground and secured Cabbie firmly in place.

"Ready?" Jimmy asked.

"Ready," said Cabbie.

Jimmy pressed the winch button again.

It took less than thirty seconds to drag Sammy free. "Yes!" shouted Cabbie. "We did it! That was brilliant."

The screen on Cabcom lit up to show that Sammy was trying to make another call, and this time Jimmy answered it.

Sammy's smiling face appeared. "Jimmy, Cabbie, thank you," said Sammy. "I should have trusted you."

"No problem," said Jimmy. "Now we need to help the other two and then get ourselves out of here. That block of ice could come toppling down any moment."

With Maximus and Lightning now free, there was more room to manoeuvre. Next came Dug and Chip. The combined efforts of Cabbie's roto-blade with Dug's own dextrous arm with a scoop on the end helped them to make short work of getting the digger-bot free.

That just left Missy and Monster trapped.

They had almost forgotten about the danger they were in when an ear-splitting crack echoed overhead. Jimmy looked up to see a two-metre dagger of ice hurtling down towards them.

"Look out!" he yelled into the Cabcom at the top of his lungs. All of the freed racers took evasive action, moving out of the way just in time as the icicle struck the ground where they had just been, shattering into a thousand tiny pieces.

"That was mighty close," came Chip's voice over the Cabcom. "Looks like we're gonna need to work faster and quieter, y'all. So let's get this thing done."

Without another word, and with their power as low as they could, Cabbie, Dug and Lightning circled Monster, digging and ploughing and chipping her free from the snow.

"If we can just shift a little more of this snow, Monster should be able to pull herself out," said Jimmy. "Come on, Cabbie. We need to get this done before that ice comes crashing down."

"How's it looking, Missy?" whispered Jimmy into Cabcom.

"Good," mumbled Missy, Jimmy could tell she was doing her best to talk quietly, something that was hard for the larger-than-life Australian girl. "Another couple of minutes and I should be clear," she said.

The glacier creaked above them. Another two-metre ice spear dropped, lancing into the snowdrift just a few paces from Lightning.

"Fire up your engines, Missy," gasped Jimmy. "I don't think we've *got* another couple of minutes. You've got to try and pull yourself out *right now.*"

Before Jimmy had even flicked Cabcom off, Monster's engines roared into life. The tops of her huge tyres started turning, sliding, edging forward, then rolling backwards as they buffeted against the solid wall of snow and ice encasing them.

"Come on," muttered Jimmy to himself through clenched teeth.

Again, Missy opened up Monster's throttle and battered against the snow. She climbed up half a metre and almost made it out onto the flat, but slipped and rolled back again.

"Come *on*," hissed Jimmy again, sweat trickling down the back of his neck.

"Nearly there," came Missy's voice over Cabcom, just as a deafening rumble came from the glacier.

Up came Monster again, pushing up and on and out of the snow – and suddenly she was free!

Jimmy would have cheered, but there was no time. "Quickly, everyone," he yelled into Cabcom. "Let's go, go, *go*!"

There was a roar of engines. They were all past worrying about making too much noise. Missy and Monster lurched forwards, smashing a gap through the left side of the snowdrift, closely followed by Maximus and Sammy, Lightning and Kako, Dug and Chip and, lastly, Jimmy and Cabbie.

"It's breaking off!" Cabbie shouted. And he was right. The house-sized block of ice finally slid from its perch at the top of the glacier and tumbled over the edge.

There was a whistling sound as it sliced through the air and fell down, down, down – right towards Jimmy and Cabbie.

"Aaaaaaahhhh!" Jimmy yelled as his foot squashed the accelerator. "Go, Cabbie!"

BOOOOOOMMMMM!

Cabbie was tossed into the air by the shock waves as the ice block smashed through the track just a few metres behind them. He skidded as he landed, his tyres screeching in protest. For a moment Jimmy thought he would swerve straight back into the ocean, but he managed to catch the slide and steer Cabbie back to the centre of the track.

Only then did he dare look in his rear-view mirror.

It looked like something out of a disaster movie. The whole section of track had disappeared behind them and the icy surface had been smashed into little pieces, which fizzed and frothed in the ocean.

"We did it, Cabbie!" Jimmy cheered.

"And just in time," the robot replied. "I think my nerves have blown a gasket."

"That," said Grandpa, his beaming face popping up on the Cabcom, "was incredible. I haven't been so frightened and excited all at once since the first time I took the stabilizers off your bike."

Jimmy could feel his face going red. "Oh, Grandpa!"

he blushed.

"A marvellous effort, my boy, marvellous!" said Grandpa. "See you at the finish line."

The Cabcom went silent.

"Well," said Cabbie, "you had me worried for a minute back there."

"Me too," said Jimmy. "But we don't have any time to waste. There's still a race to be won and we've only got a little time to catch Horace and the rest of them."

"No problem, Jimmy. I'll shift all power to the engines and we'll be right back in this r—" Cabbie suddenly went silent.

"What's the matter, Cabbie," Jimmy asked, looking worried.

"I've got some bad news," the robot said. "I've just detected a puncture to my back tyre."

CHAPTER FIFTEEN
Last

"What's happened? Can we fix it?" Jimmy asked. He had a sick feeling in his stomach, like he'd eaten a whole pack of rotten eggs.

"Normally, yes. Your grandpa fitted an automatic re-inflation device, but I can't work it. There's an icicle stuck in the tyre. In fact, it's pierced all the way through to the wheel."

Jimmy was silent for a second. Then he said, "So what now?"

"We'll just have to limp to the finish," Cabbie said. "Sorry, Jimmy."

Jimmy racked his brains, but there was nothing

he could think of that would save them. He jammed his foot down on the accelerator a little harder. The steering wheel squirmed in his hands as the flat tyre wibbled and wobbled dangerously. The finish line was so close that he could almost touch it, but there was nothing else they could do but watch through the zoom screen as the others finished the race. He thumped the steering wheel in frustration. "Of all the reasons for losing a race … a puncture!"

Up ahead Missy and Monster were barging past Chip and Dug, who then pushed their way back to the front again, nearly sending Kako and Lightning off the ice track and into the snowdrifts. Maximus followed, swerving left and right, trying to find a way through.

"Finish line in five hundred metres," announced Cabbie.

"Too late!" Jimmy sighed as he saw Monster and Missy racing over it. Chip and Dug followed soon after, then Kako on Lightning and Sammy in Maximus just behind. But Horace had finished long before them all. He'd built up too much of a lead on the others after the avalanche and he was already out of Zoom, leaning on the bonnet of his robot with a smirk that stretched from ear to ear.

Jimmy thought about the zero points he would get for finishing last, and felt a lump in his throat.

I could have won this race so easily, he thought to himself. *But then, what would have happened to the others? They might never have escaped that snowdrift.*

"Never mind, Jimmy," said Cabbie, as if he had read Jimmy's thoughts. "The important thing is that you did the right thing. I bet there's never been a robot racer who's done something more selfless than what you did today."

"Thanks, Cabbie ... There's always next time, I suppose," Jimmy murmured as they drove as fast as they dared across the line in last place. When they came to a standstill, Jimmy took a deep breath and let out an enormous sigh.

"Sorry, Jimmy," said Cabbie. "I did my best."

Tired and disappointed, Jimmy climbed out of Cabbie's cockpit. Slowly he became aware of something going on above him, and he raised his head to the big screens hanging from the grandstands on either side. Each of the giant TVs showed the image of him stood next to Cabbie. He couldn't help noticing that the image made him look even more exhausted than he felt.

Strange, he thought. *The camerabots are always focused on the winner after the races.* But as he slowly took in the scenes within the finishing paddock, he couldn't help but notice that every lens was trained on him. And every steward, mechanic, and race official was clapping and cheering him.

Then he heard the commentator yelling over the noise, "Ladies and gentleman, I give you the hero of the race … *Jimmy Roberts.*"

Jimmy couldn't help smiling. He gave a little wave to the camera, and a shy smile, before making his way slowly to where the other racers had gathered. *Perhaps winning isn't everything, after all*, he thought to himself.

Just then Jimmy caught sight of the one person he didn't want to see. Horace Pelly was wandering over to him, a broad smile of triumph on his smug face.

"I was wondering where you lot had got to," said Horace. "I came across the finish line about twenty minutes ago – which, I think, makes me the winner.

And which, if I'm not much mistaken, makes me the winner of an amazing Leadpipe Industries upgrade!"

Jimmy looked to his left and to his right. He found himself standing in between Princess Kako, Missy, Chip and Sammy. All of them were staring angrily at Horace.

"What's wrong?" asked Horace.

"What's wrong?" bellowed Missy in disbelief. "*What's wrong?*"

"Yes, you have won this race, Horace," said Sammy, "but do you know what danger you caused for the rest of us?"

"I can't help it if you losers get yourselves stuck, can I?" Horace smirked.

"But you sure didn't need to put us all in danger, did you, mate? That stunt of yours could have brought down the whole flamin' glacier!" bellowed Missy. "You're as dumb as they come, Horace Pelly. You should be ashamed of yerself."

"We could all have been killed out there today if it hadn't been for Jimmy," Chip added.

"Now, come on, everyone, let's not get carried away," said Horace. "Besides, he's not perfect

– you should have seen the stunt he pulled on me earlier on."

Jimmy felt a burst of shame. He stepped forward in front of everyone and looked at Horace. "I'm really, really sorry about that," he said seriously. "I'll never do anything like that again."

Horace snorted. "Whatever, *loser*," he sneered.

Joshua Johnson, the robot co-ordinator, appeared on the other side of the pit area, dancing from foot to foot in his blue blazer, yeti trousers and furry brown boots. He was waving his clipboard urgently. "Horace?" he called. "Horace, if you could stop chatting with your friends and come to the winners' rostrum, please? And…" He consulted his clipboard. "Missy? Chip? Could you come too, please?"

"Hear that, Jimmy?" Horace grinned. "The *winners'* podium. That would be the podium for winners. Not losers like you."

As they made their way over to the awards ceremony, the camerabots surged around. Lord Leadpipe stood on the rostrum with a microphone, his monocle glinting from the depths of his fur-lined hood. It almost looked like he was relieved that this race was over. He looked very tired as he announced the top three in reverse order.

"In third place with six points," he said, his voice echoing in the wind, "Chip Travers and Dug." Lord Leadpipe presented Chip with a wreath of leaves. Unsure whether to wear it on his head or round his neck, Chip waved his wreath at the cameras.

"In second place for eight points," continued Lord Leadpipe, "Missy McGovern and Monster." Missy perched her wreath on her head and pogoed up and down.

"And in first place, taking the maximum ten points," said Lord Leadpipe, "Horace Pelly and Zoom."

Horace stepped up onto the podium with his hands in the air, waving at the camerabots. But the atmosphere had suddenly gone flat. Jimmy thought he might even have heard one or two people booing. Horace didn't seem to notice. He grinned with his huge white teeth and winked at the cameras. Then he turned to face Lord Leadpipe expectantly.

"And as the winner of the Arctic Adventure, Horace," continued Lord Leadpipe, "I am particularly proud to present you with a very special prize from

Leadpipe Industries." Horace's face lit up. Lord Leadpipe beckoned to Joshua Johnson, who climbed onto the podium holding something covered in purple cloth. Horace held out his hands in expectation.

Lord Leadpipe took hold of the cloth and whisked it away like a magician revealing a dove in a cage. But it wasn't a dove in a cage. Joshua was holding a red velvet cushion with an object resting on it. Lord Leadpipe lifted the object from the cushion and ceremoniously handed it to Horace.

The crowd fell silent.

"This," said Lord Leadpipe, "I am very proud to say, has been specially created to commemorate fifty years of Leadpipe Industries." He handed it to Horace.

Horace stared at it for a moment. Then he stared at Lord Leadpipe. "What is it?" demanded Horace.

"That," said Lord Leadpipe, "is a piece of lead pipe, taken from the very first processing plant where I began—"

"A piece of lead pipe?" repeated Horace in horror.

"Yes," said Lord Leadpipe.

"A piece of pipe?" repeated Horace in disbelief. "Made of lead?"

"You must be very proud," said Lord Leadpipe, grabbing Horace's limp hand and pumping it up and down like a piston.

Horace just stared at him, his arm limp against the vigorous handshake.

Jimmy could see Missy trying to hide a smile. "*It's just a bit of old pipe,*" she mouthed to the other racers, stifling a giggle. Sammy snorted with laughter, but managed to cover it up as a cough. And Chip was grinning broadly. They all knew how much Horace had wanted a fancy upgrade – and how much he would have gloated about using it in the next race. Even the quiet and usually straight-faced Kako broke into a smile.

Sensing an outburst from Horace at any moment, Joshua Johnson hurriedly hustled him and Lord Leadpipe from the podium.

As the ceremony came to a close, Jimmy spotted Grandpa. He ran to give him a hug.

"Did you see Horace, Grandpa?"

Grandpa nodded and smiled. "I did, my boy. I don't think that Horace Pelly really understands sentimental value, does he?"

"It doesn't look like it," Jimmy replied with a grin.

"Anyway, I'm proud of you, boy," said Grandpa as they headed back to Cabbie. "You didn't win this one, but you showed enough courage for ten robot racers."

"Thanks, Grandpa," smiled Jimmy, glowing with happiness.

"And," continued Grandpa, "you're still at the top of the leaderboard with young Chip on eighteen points. It's getting tight with that good-for-nothing Horace Pelly just behind you on sixteen points, along with Princess Kako, then it's Missy on fourteen points and Sammy on twelve."

That made Jimmy feel even better. He'd had his worst race yet, but he was still in with a shot.

"Excuse me, gentlemen," growled a voice.

Jimmy turned to find Pete Webber smiling at them.

"That was an incredible race," said Pete in his deep rumbling voice. "You made a big mistake with that robo-pummeller, but – you know what? – Big Al sometimes gets carried away like that. He can't think about anything but winning. But like you he always does the right thing in the end," he nodded, adding "usually" under his breath.

"Thanks, Pete," said Jimmy, his cheeks burning with pride. He loved it when Pete compared him to Big Al. "Will you be back working with us for the next race?" he asked.

"Don't know," growled Pete. "I'd love to, but ... I'll have to talk to Lord Leadpipe and see what he—"

"Did I hear my name?" said a voice. Lord Leadpipe was strolling over to them, his yeti-like trousers swinging madly as he moved. He put a friendly arm round Pete's shoulders and leaned into their conversation. "Something about Pete helping you with Cabbie?" he said. "Well," he went on, putting his other arm round Jimmy so that he had them both in an embrace, "I can't tell you how proud I am of you, Jimmy. You were immensely brave in helping your fellow competitors when their lives were in danger. I would never have forgiven myself if something had happened today. But thanks to you, each one of them is still in one piece."

Lord Leadpipe looked deep into Jimmy's eyes and Jimmy could see that the billionaire was being deadly serious.

"I can't say I've ever seen anyone risk so much to protect others and sacrifice their own chances," Lord Leadpipe went on. Then a smile crept onto his face, "And bravery of that kind certainly deserves some kind of reward. But," he said, "much as I would like to, Jimmy, I can't bend the rules and give you the points you deserve. So I think the least we can do is lend you Pete Webber for a couple of weeks. If that's OK with you, Pete?"

"It sure is," said Pete, his little black eyes crinkling with pleasure.

"And would that be agreeable with you, Wilfred?" asked Lord Leadpipe.

Grandpa, who had been quietly staring at the ground since Lord Leadpipe appeared, looked up and smiled. "Of course!" he exclaimed. "You're welcome anytime, Pete. The kettle's always on!"

"Great," said Pete.

"You mean—" began Jimmy, who had finally managed to open his mouth and speak.

"— you mean Pete Webber – *the* Pete Webber – is going to be working with us for two whole weeks?"

"If it's OK with you, Jimmy?" smiled Pete.

"OK?" cried Jimmy. "OK? It's more than OK. It's …
amaaaazing!"

Pete laughed and patted him on the back.

"Oh, and one more thing," said Lord Leadpipe,
leaning in conspiratorially. "There was a second
special prize today, but seeing as my first offering was
received with so little enthusiasm, I think it needs a
different home. I think it should go to the hero of the
race. Here you go." And with a wink he passed a small
parcel to Jimmy.

Jimmy stood rooted to the spot. What could this
package be?

"Open it, my dear boy – we don't have all day,"
Lord Leadpipe encouraged him.

"Go on then, Jimmy. Open it and see what it is,"
Grandpa said. Even he couldn't hide his curiosity.

Carefully, Jimmy unwrapped the parcel to see a fat
metal tube.

Pete's mouth dropped open as he looked at it. "Is
that…?" he breathed.

"A sonic-booster," Leadpipe said proudly. "Latest
Leadpipe technology. Should be even faster than
those rocket-boosters you've got, Jimmy."

"Cabbie's going to *love* it," Jimmy grinned. "Thank you, Lord Leadpipe. I don't know what to say."

"There's nothing to say, Jimmy. You deserve it more than anybody … as you will see from the inscription on the side."

Jimmy turned the booster over and read the engraving out loud: "*For a true racing spirit.*"

Lord Leadpipe grinned at Grandpa. And for once, Grandpa smiled back at him.

"That's quite some grandson you have, Wilfred," Lord Leadpipe said. "He's got a lot of fans rooting for him now, I believe. I expect a good performance when you next take to the track, Jimmy."

"Oh, don't you worry about that," replied Grandpa. "My Jimmy and I will be ready to handle whatever you throw at us, won't we, my boy?"

"Of course we will," said Jimmy. "We've still got a championship to win!"

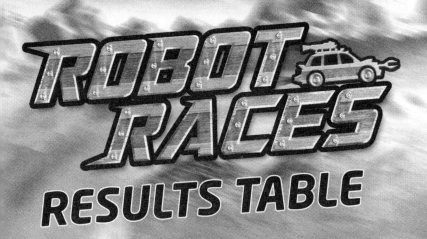

RESULTS TABLE

RACE 3: ARCTIC ADVENTURE

Race Position	Racer	Robot	Points
1	Jimmy	Cabbie	18
1-	Chip	Dug	18
3	Kako	Lightning	16
3-	Horace	Zoom	16
5	Missy	Monster	14
6	Sammy	Maximus	12

Turn over for a sneak peek of the next Robot
Races adventure ... *DESERT DISASTER*

DESERT DISASTER

"On your marks ... get set ... *go!*" shouted Princess Kako.

Jimmy Roberts reached for a packet of crisps from the table and popped it open with one hand. Beside him, Chip Travers did the same.

Opposite them sat Missy McGovern and Sammy Bahur, each with their hands clasped behind their backs and their mouths open wide like two seals at feeding time.

"Incoming!" Jimmy shouted to Missy as he started throwing salty crisps at her mouth as quickly as he could, while Chip did the same to Sammy. The crisps were bouncing off noses, ears and cheeks as Missy and Sammy weaved to and fro, fighting to catch as many in their mouths as they could.

"Come on, Sammy," yelled Chip. "We can't afford to lose this game."

"Iiimm-ooeein-mmiii-eeeessss!" the Egyptian boy replied, which Jimmy thought translated into, "I'm doing my best!"

"Time's up," said Kako suddenly. "Everybody stop what you're doing. Close your mouths and put down the snacks!"

The room fell silent apart from the dull noise of food being chewed.

"I think we won that one, don't you, Jimmy?" said Missy, shaking crumbs from her hair.

"Are you kidding me?" said Chip. "We caught more chips than you! Kako, who won?"

"I was too busy laughing!" the Japanese princess replied.

Jimmy smiled and shook his head as the jokey squabble carried on. Missy had come up with the game and it had had the entire group laughing the whole way through their lunch hour.

Jimmy plucked a sandwich from the table and

popped it into his mouth. He was reaching for his drink when he noticed that the liquid in the glass was tilting at an unusual angle. It was the only sign that he was actually suspended thousands of metres in the air on an enormous airship owned by none other than the famous billionaire Lord Ludwick Leadpipe. The water rolled up the right side of his drinking glass ever so slightly as the giant craft moved through the air.

Jimmy loved being part of the first-ever Robot Races for kids. He loved the danger, the excitement and visiting new places. But the competition had become so popular that all the racers had turned into celebrities overnight. All of a sudden, newspaper reporters wanted to know everything about them, and had started standing on their doorsteps with camera crews day and night to catch a glimpse here and a quick word there. Grandpa had got so fed up with them turning up at his door that he'd rigged the doorbell to squirt water at whoever rang it!

Soon Lord Leadpipe had decided to take action. He converted part of his giant airship into a school, and gathered everyone on board to live there for the duration of the Races.

The luxury airliner had everything – classrooms, science labs, and a canteen that was bigger than the one at Jimmy's school. Leadpipe had hired a tutor to teach them all the usual subjects like maths and science, but he'd also arranged for them to be taught a few *special* lessons. They were being taught basic mechanics, advanced driving skills and interview techniques – all things they'd need to be top robot racers.

Looking around the table at the other competitors, Jimmy still couldn't believe he was now living aboard a giant airship that could travel at supersonic speeds, with its own luxury en-suite cabins, a fancy restaurant, cinema, and even a bowling alley. It was completely different from the run-down house in Smedingham where he had been brought up by his grandpa. The same grandpa who had also turned out to be a genius robot inventor and engineer – when he wasn't busy being a taxi driver.

Around Jimmy were the other robot racers. They were all kids like him, taking part in the biggest, most exciting tournament the world had ever seen – each with their own robot equipped with the finest gadgets and technology. They were friends now, but on the track they'd be fighting each other for first place.

First there was Princess Kako from Japan. She and her robobike, Lightning, were serious contenders in the Robot Races championship, having already won one stage of the competition. Lightning was light and fast, usually shaped like a motorbike – although he could transform into lots of other vehicles when needed – and was propelled by two turbo jets.

Next came Chip Travers. Chip's racer was called Dug, and he was a giant diggerbot with a large hydraulic arm that had come in handy a few times in the tournament. They'd been friends since Jimmy had rescued Chip from the Grand Canyon in their first race together.

Opposite Chip sat Samir – or Sammy, as he liked to be called – a skinny boy from Egypt who came from a long line of successful racing drivers. His father, Omar Bahur, had been a champion robot racer in his day, leaving Sammy a lot to live up to. His robot was called Maximus, and was a huge hovercraft able to glide at top speed on a cushion of air over almost any surface.

"I have never seen such arguments over a snack

before," whispered Sammy to Jimmy as Missy and Chip continued their debate. "It is almost as if this game is as important as the Robot Races, no?"

Jimmy laughed. "I think we're all a bit *competitive*, Sammy."

Missy turned to the two of them and laughed. "Crikey, Sammy, if you think this is competitive, you should see me and my bro when we have our speed shearing contests – you've never seen so many sheep trimmed so quickly."

Jimmy couldn't help liking the loud, confident tomboy. She lived in the Australian Outback and was an expert at tackling difficult terrain with her giant robotruck Monster. Jimmy liked Missy's sense of humour and the mad games she came up with.

"That wasn't in the rules!" Missy shouted now, a smile on her face.

"You made up the rules two minutes ago!" argued Chip. "Jimmy, whose side are you on?"

"Whoa, keep me out of it!" Jimmy laughed. "You'll have to fight it out yourselves."

Just then the door slid open and Horace Pelly walked in, his tray overloaded with food.

"Hey, Horace!" said Chip cheerily.

Horace ignored him, heading for a different table where he sat down with his back to the group.

Horace was the only robot racer Jimmy had known before the competition started, although he wouldn't exactly have said they were friends. In fact, Jimmy had mixed with the school show-off about as well as cornflakes went with pickled onions ... not very well at all!

Jimmy shook his head as he thought about life back in the little town of Smedingham. He wondered what his best friend Max was doing now, and if Max missed seeing him at all. Sometimes he wished that Max could be on the airship too. It would be great to show him round the workstations, the swimming pool and the games room on board.

Jimmy popped a slice of tomato in his mouth and looked over at Horace. He sighed. "*Treat others the way you'd want to be treated,*" was what Grandpa always said, and Jimmy knew that sitting on your own was no fun.

"Hey, Horace," he called over. "There's a space at our table if you want to eat with us."

Horace gave a snort of laughter and turned to Jimmy with a sneer on his face.

"With you? No thanks!" he said. "I don't fraternize with the competition. And keep the noise down, will you? This place sounds like the zoo at feeding time."

Jimmy's face turned red. *I should have known he'd throw it back in my face*, he thought. He opened his mouth to talk to Princess Kako, but just at that moment a loud blare came from the other side of the room.

Horace had switched the television on, and the Robo TV theme tune sang out at full volume. Jimmy hadn't even known there was a TV in the canteen, but when he turned to look he saw that one of the large white walls was actually a giant plasma screen. He recognized the presenter immediately – it was Bet Bristle, an elderly but lively interviewer he had first met before the Rainforest Rampage race. Up on the massive TV, her usually dainty little nostrils were the size of dinner plates.

"Welcome to another edition of *Full Throttle*, the Robo TV show that lifts the bonnet of the Robot Races and takes a good look inside." Bet announced.

"I hope they don't look under Cabbie's bonnet," joked Jimmy. "Grandpa left his toolkit under there last week!"

"Shhh!" said Horace.

"We've got a great show for you this week!" Bet continued. "So stay tuned!"

Read *DESERT DISASTER* to find out
what happens next!

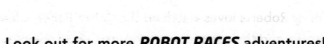

Look out for more *ROBOT RACES* adventures!

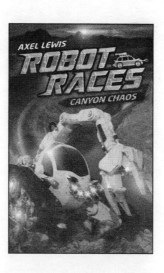

Jimmy Roberts loves watching the Robot Races, where drivers and their super-smart talking robots compete. When a new race for kids is announced, Jimmy is desperate to join in. There's only one hitch – he'll never be able to afford a robot. All Jimmy can do is watch while his worst enemy, Horace Pelly, boasts about the robot NASA are building him.

But then Jimmy's grandpa reveals that he hasn't always been a taxi driver. In fact, he might be the only person who can help – by turning his battered old taxicab into a real-life robot!

Will Jimmy and his robot Cabbie ever be able to keep up with the competition?

Jimmy and Cabbie are ready for the next race in the
championship – a daring dash through the deepest,
darkest, jungle. Cabbie's new gadgets might give him
an edge, but will he let his fear of snakes hold him back?
Jimmy's friend Sammy and his hovercraft robot, Maximus,
are right behind them, so every second counts.

**With arch-enemy Horace up to his usual
tricks, will Jimmy even finish the race?**

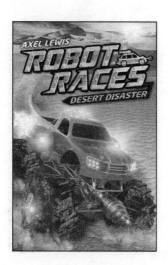

The adventure through the sweltering Sahara desert is a
race with no track! Missy and her huge robot, Monster,
are used to racing in the Australian outback, but even
they are stumped when the robots and their racers have
to solve clues to find the right direction. It will take brains
as well as gadgets to reach the finish line!

**Can Jimmy and Cabbie surf the sand dunes
and finish first?**

For more exciting books from brilliant

authors, follow the fox!

www.curious-fox.com